SURVIVOR

ROSS GREENWOOD

Boldwood

First published in 2017. This edition first published in Great Britain in 2022 by Boldwood Books Ltd.

Copyright © Ross Greenwood, 2017

Cover Design by Nick Castle Design

Cover Photography: Shutterstock

The moral right of Ross Greenwood to be identified as the author of this work has been asserted in accordance with the Copyright, Designs and Patents Act 1988.

All rights reserved. No part of this book may be reproduced in any form or by any electronic or mechanical means, including information storage and retrieval systems, without written permission from the author, except for the use of brief quotations in a book review.

This book is a work of fiction and, except in the case of historical fact, any resemblance to actual persons, living or dead, is purely coincidental.

Every effort has been made to obtain the necessary permissions with reference to copyright material, both illustrative and quoted. We apologise for any omissions in this respect and will be pleased to make the appropriate acknowledgements in any future edition.

A CIP catalogue record for this book is available from the British Library.

Paperback ISBN 978-1-80280-381-5

Large Print ISBN 978-1-80280-380-8

Hardback ISBN 978-1-80280-379-2

Ebook ISBN 978-1-80280-383-9

Kindle ISBN 978-1-80280-382-2

Audio CD ISBN 978-1-80280-374-7

MP3 CD ISBN 978-1-80280-375-4

Digital audio download ISBN 978-1-80280-376-1

Boldwood Books Ltd
23 Bowerdean Street
London SW6 3TN
www.boldwoodbooks.com

To Uncle Alan and Auntie Ricky. Lovely people.

They called me Eighteen, but I didn't do it.

— VINCENT ROACH

In the end, the only judgement that matters is that of your children.

— VINCENT'S MOTHER

I did what had to be done.

— VINCENT'S FAMILY MOTTO

1

FIFTY YEARS AGO

I was born. My mum told me that I began life quietly, with barely a murmur. I will leave the same way.

1966 was the year England won the World Cup. When I look back, it sometimes feels as though it was downhill after that. And I don't even like football.

2

1980 – AGE: 14

The silence lasted at least a minute before anyone spoke.

'Had a stroke of what?'

I looked over at Frank and stopped the same question falling out of my mouth.

'No, he's had a stroke,' my mum said.

My brother's eyes narrowed in confusion. He glanced at me for help, but my slack face displayed the same ignorance.

'It's like a heart attack, but in your brain,' she finally answered.

It sounded serious, but I found it hard to connect the words to my dad. He was a big, strong man. A dustman no less. Some of the bins, at the posh houses, had wheels but the majority had to be lifted onto your back. He'd always been an immovable presence in my family – a consistent man who grounded us. He did have kids late in life, but he'd only seen fifty a few years ago. It didn't make sense.

'Is he dead?' Frank asked.

'No, he's still alive.'

The way she said it left the chance of that finality being

distinctly possible. My brother was a simple boy. He would have been fifteen then, so perhaps a man. He saw the world in two colours: black and white. Therefore, he seemed cold but that wasn't who he was.

He just knew his position in the scheme of things, and anything that confused or threatened him he addressed forcefully and directly – until he understood it, processed it, and could place it where he had an element of control. Violence was often close by. Frank seemed a pleasant name, but the reality was different.

My mum would never get away with that loose reply.

'Is he going to die?'

'No, Frank. They don't think so, not now.'

He'd been gone a week, so we knew it was serious. I saw the ambulance leave as I got home from school that day and found our neighbour, May, waiting for me in our kitchen. Old people have strange phrases, often for every event. She said, 'Your dad's had a funny turn.' An understatement if ever there was one.

She escorted me to her house for tea, being aware Frank stayed out until late at night. May was a nice lady, but she only gave us things on toast. That would have been fine, but there were risks involved. The food could be fresh or stale. You put the edge of the toast in your mouth and nibbled, knowing it might be mouldy. As luck would have it, she had a Jack Russell who, despite our best efforts, was never sick.

My mum went in the ambulance with my dad. She only returned on the odd occasion, and then didn't stay long. I found her sobbing one morning a few days later, hunched over the sink, and I gave her a hug. She was a bird-like creature. I sometimes felt as though I could crush her, but her bones must have been made of steel. All she said was, 'He's ill, Vincent.'

I didn't know what to say; I'd never been great with dealing with extremes of emotion. None of us were – my brother in particular. His brutal nature wasn't driven by anger or anxiety, but by fact-based decision-making. That was why they feared him. However, I believed my mum would sort things out. She always did.

There was no question of going to visit. We lived on the wrong side of town from the hospital, for a start. There were buses but there was no way my dad would want us to see him like that. We didn't need to ask.

'What will happen now? When's he coming home?' I said.

'I'm not sure, Vincent. It may be some time. In the meantime, we carry on as normal. We pull together, as always.'

'No problem.'

Frank smiled and got up from his seat. He'd waste no more energy thinking about the issue until necessary. I had many more questions than that because I was almost the opposite of my brother. The world confused me. So I focused on the things I understood, like my family and the odd friend, relationships in general, and ignored the rest. As I opened my mouth to enquire about money, my mother interrupted me.

'Wash your hands. Your tea will be ready in ten minutes.'

The conversation seemed over, so I trudged upstairs to my room. Mum was always forceful in controlling my worries. I was only fourteen years old, yet concerned by adult things. I wondered whether my dad not working and being unable to pay the bills was the last thing on her mind, or the first.

I sat on the edge of my bed and did biceps curls with my weights. Not dumb-bells, they were bottles of water. I hoped they worked. I looked in the mirror – a thin boy with a scar down the centre of his forehead stared back.

They told me a car hit me when I was about seven years old, chasing a dog into the road. Both of our heads split open although only I survived. I couldn't remember it. In fact, I couldn't recall anything before that day, which unsettled me. Frank used to joke that they put the dog's brain back in my head by mistake, and everyone liked me more afterwards. I sometimes dreamt what he said was true.

Concentrating on my breathing, and trying to rid my mind of images of burning oil, bloody clothes, and mangled metal, I failed to notice my brother appear in the doorway. I stopped and braced myself for some verbal abuse.

'Keep going but slow down. It's not a race.'

'Will this make me stronger?'

'Of course. You need to do press-ups and sit-ups too. Loads of them.'

'Will it work?'

He paused, then grinned.

'No, Vinnie. That's not who you are.'

As he pulled the door shut, I realised that conversation summed up our relationship. I was in awe of him, yet often afraid. For as long as I could remember he had been giving me dead legs and thick ears. He might be cruel, aggressive and dismissive of me, but, when things were important, his concern was intermingled with warmth.

I found him consistent, if that sounds possible for someone with such strange values. I liked that. I expected nothing from him so could only be surprised, and I sometimes was. There were worries ahead though, because he's older. When he left school, I would be unprotected.

Whereas Frank's face brooked no argument, mine invited bullying. At a glance, we were similar. Neither of us appeared handsome, despite my parents saying I looked like Elvis Presley. Maybe I did after the drugs and bad advice took hold, or perhaps the day they pulled him off the toilet.

We had the features of film stars, yet they were just not quite in the right place or proportion. This made him look hard, and me soft. Despite that, only one person had ever hit me at school.

I didn't even know who he was at that point. I trod on the back of his foot in the tuck-shop queue and he elbowed me without turning around, and split my lip. He and his friends then proceeded to make my life a misery for the next few months. He was two years older and a big lad. I tried to avoid them but schools were small places.

However, not much later, I noticed that people were leaving me alone. I never saw that boy again. Even if I looked the other bullies in the eye, they glanced away. I later found out he was called John Victory. You would think great things awaited a boy with a name like that. Instead, he drowned.

This newfound freedom was a mixed gift, I suspect, given by my brother. Although no longer bullied, I struggled to make friends as now the kids were wary, when before I think most didn't know I existed.

It seemed sibling life was best explained by the ability to be evil to each other, yet to stick together when threatened. He might inflict physical or mental pain on me, but others couldn't. It would be a theme through our lives. As the years passed by, and childish games were forgotten, his loyalty would be my salvation.

3

My mum hollered up the hall.

'Tea's ready.'

I'd spent my lunch money on a magazine so raced to the top of the stairs. My brother arrived first, palmed me off, then clattered downwards. Mum waited in the dining room, slowing us up with a disapproving look, which hid affection.

We had one of those pull-out tables for our meals. The kind you wanted to push down on, even though you knew they couldn't bear the weight. Egg and chips, for the third time that week. She must have been lacking inspiration due to my dad's demise.

We sat and ate at three different speeds. This was our general approach, not because we were bored by the repetitive fare. My brother wouldn't have tasted his food, the speed he devoured it. It was just necessary fuel to enable him to get up to mischief. My mother had other things on her mind and dipped the odd chip into a greasy egg yolk. I'd always been steady as she goes.

My mum had left her *Reader's Digest* on the table, so I read that and grazed. My problems were temporarily unimportant as I immersed myself in others' lives, safe in the knowledge my dad wouldn't shout, 'None of that while we're eating.' I wasn't to know he'd never do that again, and I would pine for it.

That was perhaps the most important fact about me: I read. All the time and every chance I got. I read whilst doing my weights, swapping the book from side to side. I read before school, at breaks and during lessons if I could get away with it. It was almost like I'd become invisible to the teachers, so I could do what I liked.

My grades were okay at that point, but I was falling behind in maths and science. My general knowledge and vocabulary were vast, yet I was often referred to as an idiot. I knew I could have told my brother when that happened, but didn't as I liked the anonymity my status provided me.

People still struggled to get on with me. I understood this wasn't normal. However, I thought I was fine with it because I knew what the reasons were. I wanted to immerse myself in books and so didn't need friends. Why go bowling, or sit in the park, when there was an entire universe at your fingertips in the local library? A packet of sweets, a well-written novel, and my mind was elsewhere. Where I was sitting and who was near me were irrelevant.

I thought books were full of every kind of emotion and action. I loved to read the varieties – madness, perversion, honesty, forgiveness, and the rest, all meshed together. Life, to me, was not how my brother saw it. My world was a million shades of colour. I understood how people were different, and that was what made us alike.

I also enjoyed surprising people. We had to write a paper on John Steinbeck's *Of Mice and Men*. Bullying, fear, family and sacrifice. These were my friends. When the teacher passed the marked answers out, there was only one word at the top of mine: 'Amazing'.

My brother burped and shifted his plate forward.

'Okay, I'm off out round Billy's. Don't wait up.'

Then he walked away without even a backward glance. I wondered, with a stifled laugh, what my mum would say if I repeated what he'd said. Have a stroke like my dad, perhaps.

Billy lived in the next street. My dad called him a bruiser – not without some affection. Billy tolerated me, I think, or he had little to say. He had an air of mustiness and my mum often tried to feed him. We saw him infrequently, though, as he and Frank roamed the streets until late. For what purpose, I'm not sure.

My mum was a stoic woman before disease arrived to dismantle our lives. She had the original stiff upper lip. But my parents were a pair, all of us a team. I didn't know what would happen to our unit with a weakened part. For the first time in my life a real rumble of dread ran through me. Like a never-ending goods train.

She took my hand.

'You've always been a good boy, Vincent. No trouble at all. Don't worry.'

'Okay, Mum. I won't.'

She left her unfinished meal and stood up. I breathed in tobacco and tears as she squeezed me from behind, while I sat there frozen, holding my cutlery.

'Don't think too much. You're such a ponderer.'

'I don't think that's a word, Mum.'

'You know what I mean. You've always understood me. We'll get through it as a family.'

I believed her. The first of many mistakes.

4

1981 – AGE: 15

My dad came home on a cold January morning, six months later. I was in my room reading a book set in Russia. Our council house contained four bedrooms, so my brother and I had our own, and there was even one for guests. Unused, of course. We never had a great deal of money, although I can't remember wanting for anything.

It was true I had some strange, ill-fitting, second-hand clothes. We did have a car, an old Cortina, but we hadn't ventured abroad like a few of the other kids at school. We enjoyed food and each other. I read books – what else was there?

'He's here, Vinnie. Come on.'

'Just finishing this last page, Frank.'

It surprised me that he waited because he struggled to keep still for a second. I found it hard to maintain concentration on the page and gave up. I was missing something anyway. Despite what I'd heard, I found *Anna Karenina* exhausting.

I inserted the bookmark, placed the novel on my desk and turned to look at Frank. His eyes moved away from mine, and he swallowed.

On my brother's face, for a few seconds, I saw fear. I patted his shoulder, and then he let me go down the stairs first. That morning was never forgotten. Not because what remained of my dad came home, but instead, that day our brotherly relationship changed.

We watched as they wheeled him out of the ambulance. He was no longer a big man. I think that was what scared Frank. He didn't know how to deal with the changes. Maybe he didn't even know what questions to ask.

He'd been due out of the hospital months beforehand but had suffered a T.I.A. I'd learnt that was a mini-stroke and it was a bad sign. He'd been making good progress until then. I'd found it almost interesting. It was as if the body had short-circuited, and we watched as his system righted itself and made new connections. The T.I.A. came when he was still too weak, and it seemed to be more like a bomb had gone off inside him.

As you might imagine, by this point I'd become a dangerous expert, having consumed every piece of reading material on the topic I could get my hands on. The outlook for him was poor. Apart from a weak heart, he was also paralysed down one side, had trouble swallowing and talking, and, perhaps worst of all, he was depressed.

I stepped forward and took the handles of the chair and pushed him around to the rear of our house. My mum had regularly been down the council to get the things she felt we needed. They were reluctant at first but soon realised it was best to give her what she wanted.

Someone from the welfare had arranged for a ramp to be built so we wouldn't have to lift him over the back step. I wheeled him through the kitchen and straight into the lounge. They had removed the internal doors too, so he could fit in each room. My brother flapped around, asking the drivers if they wanted a brew.

He made them one as they took my mum into what used to be our dining room to discuss our futures.

In the lounge, I turned the telly on and grinned at my dad. Half of his face smiled back. It was different. He had a glint in his eyes I hadn't seen since he went to the rehabilitation place. He was pleased to be home.

He'd learnt to communicate with his right hand by pointing, gesturing, and nodding. My mum and I picked it up quickly. After all, there were only so many things he could want.

He would write it down if we didn't understand. That took ages. His writing was terrible, although my mum said it wasn't much better beforehand. He wrote 'hate clean piss' once when he lay in hospital. It was the smell of urine and disinfectant.

I flicked through the channels, waiting for him to tip his chin. *Columbo* got a right-handed thumb up.

'Mum wants you,' Frank said at the door.

I stood up to leave, and my dad coughed. I turned to him and knew he wanted to show his gratitude and love. So, reaching across him, I gave him a strong reassuring hug. I felt his good arm on my back, light, yet warm. He peered at Frank, who returned his stare for a second, and then they both looked away.

Frank followed me out as though scared to be left alone in there. I suppose knowledge was power. I also saw what troubled him.

My parents were always hugging me. A touch said a thousand words. My mum in particular was tactile. Little Elvis, she called me when I was young due to my natural quiff, and she often tousled it. I doubt most parents have favourites, but I do believe they love their children in different ways. Not more or less, just in the way they interact with them.

My mum admired my brother in the same manner I suspect

the person who invented dynamite enjoyed his creation – with care, respect, and pride, but from a distance.

My dad showed his affection to Frank with bone-crushing holds and general grappling. I think he secretly got some pleasure from the odd visit from the police or the calls from the school, as nothing seemed to stick. Frank was a natural leader, but at home he appreciated the fact he wasn't the alpha male. With us, he could just be.

He used to arm-wrestle my dad, who would feign losing, his hand shaking. Then, with a roar, my dad would pick up my brother with his other arm and throw him around like he was made of cotton. There would be no more of that.

My parents loved us both for what we were – opposite ends of the spectrum. The stroke hadn't altered how I fitted in with the family, but it was obvious to me that Frank felt unsure. My mum, as usual, attacked things head-on.

'Right, boys. Sit down.'

We sat on my dad's bed and faced her. She wriggled on his commode chair to get comfortable. A smile crept onto her face and we laughed.

'I'm glad we can still giggle. The ambulance has gone, so it's just us now. I've talked to your father about what he wants, but you two can help decide how we go forward.'

She composed herself and continued.

'We have been allocated a carer, but they won't be here much of the time. However, you're aware your dad is a private man and would be uncomfortable around strangers. He can go to the toilet himself although he'll need a helping hand onto the seat. This chair is for everything. He will need food preparing and some help to eat it. He can't dress himself yet, for obvious reasons. That will be one of the hardest jobs. I think I can do most of it myself otherwise.'

'I'll be here for whatever needs doing.'

'Let me finish, Vincent. Money is tight. Both of you may need to get a part-time job to help out. We get a bit of cash from the government, so we can see if that's enough. I got the cleaning job I went for at the school. It's between four and seven every evening. Perhaps you could take turns as you will need to be responsible for him while I'm not here.'

The look on Frank's face was known the world over. General Custer would have worn the same expression as the three-thousandth Indian rode into view. He blurted his words at us.

'I'll get a job and help out like that.'

I nodded. I wouldn't have had it any other way.

5

1982 – AGE: 16

I could have counted how often I'd been on a train on one hand and still had enough fingers remaining for the number of times my dad had left the house since he became ill. Yet there we were, to wave goodbye to my brother.

The smell of diesel and the rush of people made me excited and nervous at the same time. I didn't understand why as I wasn't going anywhere. My mum wanted to push my dad, but the wheelchair was far from state of the art. It was like guiding a trolley through sand, and was another job I had seamlessly taken to be mine.

My dad sat upright and beamed. He had regained some of his strength and speech, almost to the point of being jolly. My mum, however, seemed to have shrunk over the last year. It was as if the energy and vitality he gained were pulled directly from her reserves.

She perched on the edge of a seat and lit the ever-present cigarette. I sometimes wondered whether she did it to clear the smell of the hospital he had brought home with him. At least he hadn't smoked again.

You would think my brother would've been apprehensive about the challenges ahead. Instead, he looked relieved. Frank's O level exams had got placed firmly in the black category and he hadn't sat any of them.

He'd gone straight out and taken work to bring in a wage. He'd done anything that had come his way, from labouring to packing jobs. At the house, he'd thought of himself as a spare wheel and said as much. In his free time, he'd jogged. He would go out for hours, pounding the running shoes which were his only extravagance.

If I'd analysed it, as opposed to immersing myself in literature, I would have seen the armed forces as a natural choice for Frank. He bristled with energy and needed to let off steam. The government must have been crying out for people like him. I'd even caught him reading newspapers and watching the news, which had been unheard of beforehand. I supposed it was to keep up to date with the Falklands conflict, but I believed he'd decided to join up long before that became a motivating factor.

He was different. We all were. Unexpected events like a stroke, and the grind that came afterwards, could blow families apart, yet it drew us together.

My dad had rediscovered his love of sport. He'd played football to a good standard in his youth, only dropping it as the demands of family life became all-consuming, so he enjoyed anything that came on television.

I read in the lounge next to him or, on the days where he was too weak to get out of bed, in his bedroom downstairs. I'd begun to know the man in a way I suspected I never would have done if life had continued as before. There were big gaps in his past though. I wasn't astute, but even I could tell he omitted things as he talked.

My attendance at school had suffered, but I'd had the ultimate 'get out of jail free' card. Time had drifted. Soon, it would be me making a mess of my examinations.

As I watched my dad say his farewells and fail at sneakily trying to slip my brother a folded-up wedge of cash, I allowed myself to consider the future. It was something that was often in my thoughts.

There was no way my mother could cope on her own; she wasn't strong enough. I had given up on the weights because moving a twelve-stone dead weight around was all the exercise I desired. She would still need my help. Therefore, I wouldn't be going anywhere soon. I didn't mind so much; family came first.

My brother shook hands with both my parents. As usual, no words were necessary.

'Come on, Elvis. You can carry my bag. I'm reserving my strength for killing the enemy.'

I followed him up the platform as the train glided in. I wondered where he was going, until he stopped out of earshot of the others. Frank looked up at the station clock as he searched for the words he needed.

'You're the man of the house now.'

'You'll be back.'

'I'll send money.'

'Cool. I'll spend it on sweets.'

Only then did he smile. Frank bit down on whatever he was about to say as the whistle blew. He stepped onto the train, and I passed his kitbag to him. As soon as the door shut, he pushed the window open.

'Vinnie. I just want to say thank you. What you've done is something I never could. These words don't come easy to me, but I'll make you proud, because I'm proud of you.'

We shook hands, and then hugged – a new experience, I later recalled. I'm sure I felt tears on my cheek. Mine or his, I couldn't tell. He leaned out of the window, straightened my jacket, flicked my earlobe, and then strode into the carriage.

I returned to stand next to my contented parents. All of a sudden, it felt as if we were the only people present. The train left, he pressed his palm against the glass as he went by and we said goodbye to the past.

I heard my dad whisper, 'That's my boy.'

My arms were tired from waving, and I shoved my hands in my pockets. The money given to my brother tickled my fingers. Frank was darkness and light. I wasn't to know that then, but he would be the only one who would stick by me.

Then there were three.

6

1983 – AGE: 17

I wondered whether I was unconcerned with my future due to the fact I could see it was out of my hands, or because of a general lack of ambition. Deep down, I knew that things were unlikely to continue as they were, and so I let nature take its course. I was proven right.

My dad appeared to have plateaued with regards to his rehabilitation and, despite the lack of progress, was seemingly content. The loving relationship with my mother continued and I even heard the odd strange noise coming from his room at night.

I, too, was taking notice of sex and women, though they both seemed a foreign concept. Almost everything I learnt about the topic stemmed from books. I'm not sure James Herbert's *The Rats* was a good introduction to relationships, but there were others with a more reasonable approach.

To most of my teachers' amazement, I passed nearly all of my exams. My English teacher asked if I would continue my studies. I explained my commitments in our house and that I would see what life brought. A heart attack, as it turned out. Specifically, a series of mini ones that barely registered.

They took my dad into hospital and the doctors decided he needed a bypass. A date for surgery wasn't mentioned as it was plain to all he would never be strong enough for such an undertaking. I think they thought he would fade away, but he proved them wrong and, in the end, they let him come home.

The weeks that followed were strange. We moved his things into the lounge and waited. There was only a shadow left, but my mum would get in bed with him and they would cuddle.

They surprised me when they told me to go on holiday. The crazy bat next door had won a week in Cromer at the Hotel De Paris. Full board and quite a prize. She had been entering the competitions from my mum's old *Reader's Digest*s for years. When she found out she'd won, she gave it to my mum, saying, 'What the hell do I want to go to the beach for at my age?'

Cromer is a traditional seaside resort in Norfolk. I hadn't been before but with my general lack of having been anywhere that was not surprising. The seaside is the seaside, and, when I was feeling strong, I looked forward to a break and adventure.

'I'm not going,' I said.

My mum just smiled. 'You're going.' She beckoned me to sit next to her on the sofa. 'Do you trust me?'

'Yes, of course.'

'It's a scary thought, going away, especially on your own. It's normal to feel like that. If you don't like it there, just come back. That won't be a problem. Especially seeing as we won the prize. Be young, Vincent.'

The idea something might happen while I was away nagged at my mind but the arrival of my brother and his enthusiasm gave me the confidence to pack my things.

My brother took a week's leave for the period I was away. Basic training was over, but he remained based in the UK. He had got back in time to walk me down to the bus station, which was the cheapest method of transport to the coast.

'Have a lovely break. Not too good though. I don't want to hear you've been making sweet love to all the hot chicks staying at the hotel.'

'Will there be loads of women there?'

'Yeah, that place is well known for its dances and the mischief that occurs at them.'

The word dance sent a shimmer of worry through me. Perhaps I would be able to just watch.

'Thanks for taking the time off to help while I'm away. I wouldn't be comfortable going otherwise.'

'No problem. I think my career in the navy will be a short one.'

'What? I thought that was all you wanted. Why?'

'There was fighting which got out of hand. People were hurt.'

'That's war though. Fighting is what they pay you to do.'

'Not with each other, Vinnie.' He looked away. It was always hard to see what Frank was thinking.

'I'm sure it'll work out.'

'It's too late for that. They wouldn't give me the time off.'

'You're AWOL?'

'I did what had to be done. Enjoy yourself. I bet you'll meet some interesting people.'

Without any further comment, he walked from the bus station with an amble that told of no worries. I watched with an open mouth as he left. I couldn't help thinking that the routine and discipline would've saved him. What would he do now? I supposed it would be nice to have him home.

7

I sat on the rear seats the whole way. Only the cool kids got to sit there on school trips and I kept waiting for someone to tell me to move. I arrived at the bus station in Cromer in the early afternoon.

It was August, and warm and pleasant. I couldn't believe I was actually going somewhere on my own. My thoughts flicked from terror to excitement and back again. I figured I had to shake myself out of my stupor. There was a world out there and I wanted to see it.

After asking for directions I found the Hotel De Paris. It was on the seafront, looking out over the Victorian pier. At first glance, it seemed fantastic – moody and large. I could almost sense the stories of people's lives having happened there as I stared up at the long row of windows.

The breeze was invigorating and the sea air made me feel like running. The hotel even had a revolving door in which I went around twice before handing the letter with the prize news to the girl at reception. They knew I was coming as I needed to confirm my booking over the phone beforehand. I breathed in deeply and approached the desk.

'Congratulations on your win. Have you been here before, Monsieur Roach?'

The look on her face was impish. The half-smile didn't require an immediate response, and she widened her eyes. What was I missing? I wasn't sure if it would be good news or bad. I glanced around to see if it was obvious.

There was only me in reception, and I'd been in louder churches. The whole place appeared tired. However, I thought she should be able to tell from the clothes I had on that I was used to worse.

'Thank you. No, I haven't been here before.'

'The prize is for two. Has your partner arrived as well?'

I didn't know that, and my face burned with the knowledge. I paused to think of who I could've brought with me and came up lacking.

'It will be just me.'

Her big smile pushed up her cheeks, which made me notice her eyebrows. Her thick black hair gleamed in a tight ponytail, so those wild beasts dominated her features. Her lips were cherry red in comparison. Despite that, I realised she couldn't be much older than me.

'I run the bar through there. It is very quiet bar. Come and see. Here is your key. The porter is helping other guests so a strong man will have to help himself.'

I wasn't entirely sure whether she was flirting with me or taking the piss. I didn't think I'd ever met a French person before, as I assumed that was where she'd got her *'Allo 'Allo!* accent.

'Your dinner is at seven o'clock. I hope you enjoy it here.'

She gave me a suggestive expression that made me need the toilet. I scuttled off upstairs with a racing pulse.

My home for the next week was a clean and functional room, in keeping with the areas I walked through. Tiredness descended on me like I'd been injected with an anaesthetic when I realised, for seven days, I was free.

The only responsibility I had there was to spend the pocket money given to me by my mum. May, the neighbour, had slipped me twenty pounds too, and I felt rich. I slid into the musty covers and was asleep in seconds.

I woke with a jolt, forgetting where I was for a few seconds. The light through the windows, and a glance at my watch, confirmed I had time for a wash before dinner. My best shirt wasn't up to much but was the only reassurance I had over the nerves that tried to stop me leaving my room.

I approached the doors to the dining area, where the girl from reception waited with a grin the size of a piano keyboard.

'Sit where you like, monsieur.'

'It's Vincent,' I said. The joke revealed itself as she opened the doors.

I hadn't realised God's waiting room was on the east coast of England. When I stepped into the hall of tables, I brought the average age down by about thirty years. I was the only one there whose hair was still present and wasn't grey or purple.

There were loads of free tables, although none next to the windows. I looked at the girl and smiled. I thought of my brother's comments, tipped my head back and laughed. Only a few hours ago, a situation like that would've made me cringe. I wasn't sure who this new Vincent was, but I liked him. Judging by her grin, she did too.

'And I am Sara. I will see you soon.'

I sat in the corner at a table set for four and poured myself a glass of water. The room filled up fast and my confidence drained.

There must have been a coach turn up unless they'd been below, hiding in a secret crypt. I began to perspire.

'Are these seats free?' A doddery lady with shaking hands peered at me.

I nodded to confirm.

'Are you on your own?'

'Yes, I am.'

'Don't worry, you won't get bored with us.'

That wasn't what I was expecting to hear, and I leaned back to regard her and her sleepy-looking husband as they sat down.

'It's our wedding anniversary. Sixty years. I'm Betty. Never a cross word too. Not from me anyway. Lucky to have me, aren't you, Arnold?'

'Pardon?'

'Deaf as a post he is. Eh, Arnold?'

'Pardon?'

'Ignore him, talk to me. I'm lots of fun. Do you have grand-parents?'

'No, I never knew them.'

'Shame, shame. We're silly and wise. It's the best way to be. Ooh, look, it's Doris. Yoo hoo, Doris. Wait there, I'll come over.'

She left as a waiter arrived at our table.

'Red or white, sir?' It was me who said 'pardon' to that.

'Wine, sir?'

I hadn't been in that position before so I declined. I didn't know how much it was and felt daft asking.

'You get a bottle per night, as part of your prize.'

'He'll try the red,' Arnold said. 'Give Betty her usual, I'll educate the boy here.'

The waiter took a dark bottle off his trolley and poured a small amount in my glass. He then looked at me and raised an eyebrow. Arnold reached over, picked up the glass and swallowed it with a flourish.

'Perfect. Pour it out, my man.'

'It's good to see you here again, Mr Moore.'

'It's Arnold, call me Arnold.'

'Forty years I've been coming here and they still call me Mr Moore,' he said as the man turned to another table. I couldn't resist.

'I thought you were deaf?'

'It's like Betty says. She's silly, and I'm wise.'

Then it was him who burst into laughter.

She was right, I wasn't bored. I also began to relax. They left the table around 9 p.m., saying they were getting up early to go on a coach trip to nearby Sheringham. They insisted I sit with them the next night and then used each other for support as they left the room.

That wasn't surprising as I lost count of the G and Ts that went missing from Betty's side of the table. Arnold drank most of my bottle of wine and all of another one he bought. They were so content in each other's company. The comfort of a lifetime together must be a wonderful thing to own.

They were living in the moment, too. Almost like they had lived life, and this was a bonus. Talk of their grandchildren lit up their faces, and pride ironed out the lines. Arnold was sent back to his room to get pictures of them. It made me a little sad for the lack of extended family in my life, but we can't all be lucky.

After they'd gone, I left to go to my room and then remembered the French girl. It wasn't a surprise. Thoughts of her hadn't been far from my mind all night. Instead, I took a detour and strolled down the corridor she'd pointed earlier and found a small bar with huge windows facing the sea. The weather had deteriorated and raindrops lashed the glass. The room was empty though, even of staff.

That wasn't a problem as my stomach creaked from my first ever steak. It all felt like a relaxing daydream. The sky looked haunting, so I wandered over to enjoy the view, my shoulders dropping with the delightful sensation of no responsibilities.

I tried to picture my dad snoring in his chair, or my mum lighting a fag, eyes on the distance, while sitting on the wheelchair ramp. They were there in my mind but I could only see them like they were in an old faded photograph. It was as though time had stopped there after I left, leaving him open-mouthed and my mum's smoke frozen in the breeze as if from a small steam train.

The shock of a meaty clap on my shoulders almost ejected this evening's fare straight out of my arse and onto the carpet.

'You came. Come to the bar and talk.'

I perched on a stool, in what I hoped was a continental manner. She talked and talked. I watched; I'd never met a person like her. She sashayed and swayed behind the bar in an almost dance-like manner, yet she was big. To quote my mother; 'She had a rear you could rest a plant pot on,' and her forearms wouldn't have seemed out of place on a bricklayer. Yet, I couldn't take my eyes off her.

'Sit and drink, Vincent.'

'What is it?'

'Ricard. It will put fire inside you.'

I took a sip and grimaced, then knocked the remainder back in one go. A voice in my head told me I might need that strength later, although I wasn't sure why. I finally got to ask some of the questions I had for her.

'Why are you here, Sara?'

'Wow, you pronounce my name as though you have brain damage.'

'I'm sorry, how should I say it?'

'Sa. Ra. Said fast.'

'Why are you here, Sa Ra.'

She gave me a funny look as I mangled her name, as if I were being deliberately difficult, but continued.

'I finish my exams and I take one year to come to here. To perfect my English. I speak very well already as my grandfather was English. You can tell that, of course. He was there for the liberation of Paris in 1944 and stayed. We have a guest house in the suburbs there.

'They said my mother was conceived on that wonderful day, but I did the sums and they are, as you say, bullshitters. My great-uncle, or something like that, never left this town. A fisherman still. He got me the job here at this old people's home.'

As we laughed, she knocked another shot back. Her third in ten minutes. I sipped my second. It stayed in my mouth, seemingly unwilling to be swallowed, so I let it trickle down my throat to prevent inevitable projectile vomiting. The third one she'd poured me sat just out of view, yet I felt its presence, like a taunting mouse I daren't regard.

'Where are you from, Vincent?'

Only my mother called me Vincent; it was Vinnie with everyone else. I wondered if it was a sign of how someone felt about me.

'Peterborough.'

'Petersburg? How lovely. Is it far?'

'No, three hours by coach.'

'Did you know there is a song called "Vincent", by Don McLean?' She held my hand. 'I love it very much. It suits you.'

She looked at my remaining drink and knocked that back too.

'Come, show me if you have a nice room.'

'What about the bar?'

'It's only us who do not snore here at 10 p.m.'

I half-ran and was half dragged to my freezing room. A quick flick of the light switch revealed discarded clothes, which I guided under my bed with a foot.

'The view is good,' I began.

She dragged her T-shirt off and removed her bra, dropping them both in the doorway. My eyes bulged at the looming image.

'I know what the room is like, Vincent. I work here.'

8

The bus pulled in at the station and made us all step back from the kerb. I couldn't comprehend why she hadn't come. The dream was ending with a nightmare.

She had been distant yesterday, but we'd still been all over each other. Betty had called us giddy little goats, and I'd felt alive and engaged with the world. She'd shown me the funfair, the amusements, the pubs, and the walks. Everything had been fun. The world I'd encountered in books was real, and I didn't need them any more. I hadn't read a single page since I arrived.

I'd eaten with Betty and Arnold every night. Doris, Betty's friend, had joined us too. To my amazement, she'd drunk more than Betty. Her husband had died the previous year. She'd said it felt like he had taken half of her with him. 'Embrace life,' she'd whispered. 'The part that matters is over before you know it.'

I'd embraced Sara, like she might slip away. Sometimes three times a day. I'd danced. With her all week, and with Betty and Doris at the hotel parties on the Friday and Saturday nights. All three of them had pinched my bum.

Much to my amazement, Vincent was fun. Was it the real me,

or just someone who went on holiday? People liked him; Sara loved him. I hoped I would take him home.

The driver checked my ticket with a smile I couldn't return. I wanted to get off and sprint to the hotel but the bus was the last one I could catch. My mind strained for anything I might have missed.

The manager had come over the previous night and spoken to her whilst I was eating. I'd seen her face drop from where I was sitting. I'd assumed she was being told off. She was a terrible member of staff: late, rude, drunk, and yet the guests loved her. Afterwards, she'd said nothing.

I went to the back of the bus and looked over the seats – there was no joy finding them empty this time – and stared down the street. We didn't even have a phone at our house for her to get in touch. Would she want me to ring her? I prayed she would come. However, dark thoughts arose, and I realised that she might have thought it was better to have a clean break.

My stomach lurched as the drowning sorrow of unreturned love, which I remembered from the books I'd read, was mine to enjoy. Expose yourself to life and you reveal your weaknesses. I understood.

The bus crept away from the kerb and I took one last look back. Sara pelted along the pavement into view. People were dodging out of the way as if it were the running of the bull.

'Wait!' I bellowed.

The driver eased on the brakes.

'Just a moment, sir. My girlfriend, can I please say goodbye?'

My earnest face must have jogged a distant memory.

'Sure.'

She crushed me when I got off.

'I'm sorry. I had to ring home. It's a nightmare. My mother is diagnosed with cancer. My dad cannot cope. I've just rung them. I must go back.'

'Can you visit me?' I felt selfish, but it was the only thing my mind possessed.

'I will try, Vincent.'

The waiting bus stole my speech. We breathed hard and gazed at each other until a smile dawned on her face.

'I know, Vincent. I feel it too. You are a special person. One I will not forget.'

'I've had such a good week.'

'Me too.' She pressed her wonderful bosom against mine and kissed me with a passion I can't describe.

The driver tooted his horn.

'I will write. Starry, starry night, Vincent.'

'You never played me that song.'

'One day.'

Sara gave me another peck, and I climbed aboard the bus. She walked alongside as I moved down the rows of seats, and I watched her wave until she disappeared out of sight.

I sat down and wondered if she had my address.

By the time I arrived in Peterborough the streetlights were lit. My bag felt heavy as I dragged it from underneath the bus, heaved it onto my back and began the long walk home. I walked and my mood brightened.

Even if I never saw her again, that week was something I would carry with me for the rest of my life. Maybe that was all it could be: a flash of colour in a black and white film. A glimpse of what was out there if I was man enough to reach for it. A girl had wanted me with a passion that had taken our breaths away. I might have been naïve, but deep down I knew that, chances were, someone else would too.

There was a grain of confidence inside me that she had

watered and nurtured these last seven days. Although it had taken a long time, now I felt ready for the world.

My shoulders straightened and my stride lengthened as I reached my street. I was looking forward to seeing my family.

The back of the house was dark, and I tripped up the ramp. I edged through the empty and quiet kitchen. The muffled sound of the television in the lounge became all I could hear. I poked my head into the room, so I could surprise them.

For a few seconds, I thought they were both dead. As I got closer, I saw shallow chests rising in unison. My mum's eyes flickered open, and she hauled herself out of her seat like a hibernating bear on the first day of spring.

'Welcome home, son. You have a good time?'

She looked so rough I forgot about pleasantries.

'Are you okay? You look all-in.'

Each short sentence was a challenge for her.

'Yes, just fell asleep. You want a cuppa? Bet you're parched.'

'Sit down, I'll do it.'

She didn't need telling twice and flopped back. I pottered about in the kitchen making the tea. I hoped my dad wouldn't stir as there was only enough milk left for two. The cupboards were empty and so was the fridge. My greedy brother must have chomped the lot.

My mum's eyes edged open when I returned.

'Where's Frank?' I demanded.

Anger gave her strength.

'He's gone. The idiot was absent without leave. He told me they'd agreed to the holiday. Anyway, the police turned up when he was changing a bulb for May next door. Apparently, he'd been gone for over a month. He saw them get back in their car, came home, got his stuff and disappeared.'

'When was that?'

'The day after you went.'

'No way.' I scowled as I thought of the myriad tasks that would've left my mum to do. 'What a shit. So, you've been on your own?'

'Come on, Vincent. Give him a break, we don't know what happened.'

'No wonder you're knackered.'

'May gave me a hand.'

The thought of poor old May trying to drag my disabled father onto a commode was not helpful.

'Look, go to bed. I'll sort things here. Don't worry. I'll do a big shop in the morning.'

'I'm glad you're home, Vinnie.'

'Try not to worry. How's Dad?'

'The same.'

She shuffled past, weary, stopping to kiss me on the cheek. Not for the first time, I noticed my dad had more colour in his cheeks than she did. I sat on the seat my mum had vacated, and sipped my tea. My thoughts wandered to what now seemed a long-distant holiday.

I reached in my pocket and got my new wallet out. Sara had won it on a ten-pence grabbing game. Afterwards, she'd presented it to me. There was a Polaroid picture of us in it, the one she'd made me buy for a pound from the man who came to the hotel. She had laughed when I said it was a waste of money, yet, right then, it was the best thing I'd ever bought.

9

1984 – AGE: 18

My brother finally reappeared nine months later. They caught him after he was involved in a car crash. One of the other occupants, another deserter, died at the scene. The police arrested Frank when he was in hospital with a mild concussion.

He got six months at a Military Corrective Training Centre and was then discharged dishonourably from the navy. It turned out he wasn't suitable for the forces as the only orders he could be relied on to follow were his own. He came home and moved into his old room.

'You should go away for a few days,' Frank said. 'Have a break.'

'You can imagine my reluctance after what happened last time.'

'Big words for a removal guy.'

'At least I have a job.'

'I have an interview next week. You said yourself there's nothing to do this weekend. You've got the Cortina up and running. I'll come with you. It'll be a boys' break. I'll take blankets and we can sleep in the car if you don't get lucky. Mum's new fella said he'll give her a hand while we're away.'

'You cheeky sod. He's just a friend.'

My mum was earwigging from the kitchen. Another neighbour had been popping over. He was blatantly keen and possibly up to no good with her. I hoped so because I now knew happiness was fleeting.

I considered my options. My dad was deteriorating daily and becoming less trouble. The doctors said it was incredible he had lasted so long. I'm not sure those were the words he would've used if he could have uttered any himself.

He didn't seem to know what was going on, was rarely out of bed and often not awake. It was more like looking after a baby than a toddler. He was leaving after the weekend for a hospice. They had the right machines and trained staff. Mum felt she was letting him down, but we'd explained she'd done her part. He didn't know where he was now, or who was with him.

I'd been thinking continuously of going to Cromer and the Hotel De Paris. That was why I tinkered with the car. I thought passing my test and repairing it was taking my mind off her, but the truth was I knew I would return when it was ready.

I ruined many days and nights waiting for a letter to arrive. What I wanted never came. I wrote to the hotel, putting Sara's name on the envelope, three times. The final time, I felt stupid as my hand hovered near the post box because I'd heard nothing back. I sent it regardless. Pride seemed a small price to pay.

I considered ringing, but needed to see her face. Even if the answer she gave me wasn't what I hoped to hear, I still wanted to be with her if only for a while. I needed to go back soon. If she sorted her problems out at home and returned to finish her year at the hotel, there would only be a few more weekends before her course started at university in France. Then, she would leave again.

'Go, Vincent,' my mum said from the door.

She and Frank nodded at each other. They seemed closer then. Now that my dad didn't recognise anyone, my brother didn't mind helping out. It was me that got a job. Never think life is predictable because it's far from that. The possibilities you worry about won't be the things that blindside you.

'Fine, we'll leave at four tomorrow. I need to tax the car in the morning.'

We set off at five in the end. Frank insisted on getting Dad sorted for the evening and doing all the tasks that dragged for me after so many years. Our twin-tub washing machine must have been constructed by elves to have lasted so long. The day was waning by the time he came out to leave. Mum hugged us both with tears in her eyes.

'We're only going for a night,' I said.

'You drive carefully. Special cargo. I'm just pleased to see you doing things together.'

There wasn't any traffic that late in the day so we made quick progress. The closer we got, the more nervous I became. By the time we arrived at the outskirts I was incapable of conversation. We pulled up in the car park outside the hotel, and I loosened my grip on the steering wheel.

'Go for it, Vinnie. You need to know.'

I tried to use the revolving doors, but they juddered in their frame without moving. Feeling childish, I let myself in by the door at the side. It was still church quiet. A mop of black curls looked down at the reception desk. I crept closer, a smile lifting like an African sunrise.

She glanced up and I froze in shock. It was a man with long hair.

'Can I help, sir? Is everything okay?'

My bowels had turned to water.

'Sorry, I'm fine. I'm looking for someone who used to work here.'

'Who is it?'

'Sara, a French girl.'

'Nope, sorry. I've been here six months. All the staff are new. It shut for refurbishment before that, due to a change in management. They're Spanish.'

My brain struggled to react to the news.

'I wrote to her,' was all I could add.

The man gave me a huge grin and my hopes rose.

'Are these yours?' He passed me my three letters. 'No one knew what to do with them.'

I turned and walked away, knowing I was being rude, but a plunging sickness in my stomach made me want to curl up. I had to dodge walking sticks and strollers as the ancient army came down for their evening meal. A familiar sight came into view. Not the vision I'd dreamt of but welcome, nevertheless.

'Betty, how are you?'

There was no sign of Arnold.

'Young man,' she said as she looked right through me. 'A seat at the window, please. I never get to sit at the window.'

She turned to a younger woman with a striking resemblance to her and whispered, 'Can't they employ any English staff?'

The younger woman mouthed, 'Sorry,' to me and helped Betty into the room. I staggered outside and leaned against the bonnet of the car. Frank got out.

'You okay?'

'For the first time in my life I want to get pissed.'

He looked at me and grinned.

'I can help you with that.'

10

We eventually parked in one of the spaces at a chalet park as everywhere else seemed to be residents' parking only. It was only a ten-minute walk along the breezy cliff top back to the alcohol in town. The strange weather matched my mood.

The day had cooled and there was a sea fret coming inland from the high tide and a keen wind. It was quiet for a Saturday. No doubt the gloom had put off all except the most enthusiastic of drinkers. I would make up for them.

We bar-crawled, starting with beers, before moving to shots and spirits. It helped. My mind and body relaxed as my liver geared up for the fight ahead. However, inside, there was a small swirl of rage. I didn't know where to direct it.

We weren't religious so laying the turn of events at God's gates seemed unrealistic. It being 'one of those things' was a terrible frustration though. A bell dragged me back to the present.

'That's last orders,' Frank said. 'Something for the road, sir. Or the car, for that matter?'

More alcohol wasn't an appealing prospect, but he'd expressed his enjoyment at having a drink with his brother more than once and it seemed churlish to refuse. He returned with vigour.

'Good news, there's a nightclub open tonight. Called The Pit.'

'Sounds wonderful.'

'Yes, I wonder if it's one for bears or snakes. Maybe there will be a few chicks. Time for a couple more drinks at least. You'll be glad of them, sleeping in the car with this weather.'

It turned out it would be best described as a shit pit – a dark damp hole full of scum. There was a door next to a hotel at the top of the ramp to the beach, which opened to a long slippery set of stairs. We paid two pounds each to a pair of bouncers to get in. It went straight in one of their pockets. They were big men in their forties with world-weary expressions.

Then we entered a gloomy room with ear-splitting music booming from massive speakers. I'd be surprised if they'd ever had someone stupid enough to go in there who wasn't a local. Or, at least, one who didn't immediately leave. The din continued and it was so dingy I couldn't see what was behind the bar, but I swear all thirty eyeballs in there followed our moves.

'Jesus, Frank. Let's get out of here.'

'No way, man. Ignore these pricks. Stare them back down. What are they going to do?'

As we were outnumbered, they could more or less do what they liked. I suspected the police wouldn't be in any rush to go down there either. We would never be seen again.

Frank got us a drink and I found a seat near the door. It felt like having a final request in front of the hangman. I couldn't stop myself looking around at such open hostility. For lack of anything else to look at, I stared at the filthy floor and sipped the foul liquid.

Frank garbled a few linked-up words to me.

I thought he said, 'just turds'.

'Say that again, Frank?'

'I said, last orders?'

'Go on, but let's make it quick.'

He returned with a woman in tow. She looked old enough to be my mum, before my dad was sick anyway. I shook her hand, not wanting to get close to the dental work that was exposed by her rictus grin after the shout of, 'Juz call me Gloria.'

She leaned towards me and, for a nasty moment, I thought she was going to kiss me on the cheek, European style. Instead, she froze, her eyes opened a few more millimetres, then she tilted back the same distance behind and her eyes squinted. A technique perfected over many years to remain upright in a hurricane of drink.

They stood next to me, laughing and giggling. I knocked the rest of my spirit back in one, scanning the room as the observers gave up any pretence of staring elsewhere. Fear surged through my body as a tall youth came swaggering over. I checked our escape route and saw the two bouncers had appeared. They met my gaze and took their hands out of their pockets.

The youth scowled at Frank, then stood next to him and said something in his ear. Frank looked at his face in surprise. I saw a slight bulge in his jawline before he moved forward to reply. As he did, he crouched a little and, at the last second, pulled back. He hammered his elbow up into the unsuspecting chin in front of him.

It took about two seconds for the body to hit the floor and approximately four for the onlookers to respond. Drink-addled minds roared in protest and I involuntarily backed towards the door, as shocked as they were.

Two vice-like hands gripped my upper arms and spun me around. I saw the same happen to Frank. The bouncers slammed us through the exit, opening it with Frank's face, and propelled us up the stairs. One of them shouted, 'Run.' We didn't stop to ask where.

We sprinted along the promenade back towards where we'd parked our car. The moonless sky and swirling mist made it seem like we were in a horror movie. Maybe we were.

The initial burst of adrenaline wore off quickly and Frank lagged behind. It wouldn't have taken a genius to say it was blood loss that was tiring him. A circle of crimson spread on his shirt where it poured from his nose. Excited voices echoed out of the darkness.

'Please try, Frank. Or they'll catch us.'

I dragged him along for another hundred metres before he collapsed onto a bench. He gasped air into his lungs.

'Frank, come on.'

'Fuck that, I don't run from anyone. You go, I'll meet you at the car.'

I couldn't help but smile.

'Look at you, you're done.'

Three figures appeared out of the shadows and surrounded us. They were young and furious. Frank hauled himself to his feet and breathed hard next to me.

'Running away, were we? Got some nerve in our club. Come on, boys.'

They came forward. A voice whispered at my side.

'Too drunk to run, not to brawl.'

He growled and met two of them straight on, wild fists swinging from drunken angles. The man who spoke stepped towards me and grabbed me by the throat, shoving me against the wall. I didn't want to fight, I never had. I don't think I knew how.

As the back of my head hit the concrete behind me, the ball of swirling fire in my core that had been spinning all night exploded. Frustration and rejection seized his collar in reply. We understood at the same time that they were a powerful combination. That, combined with years of heavy lifting, meant the odds weren't fair.

His expression opened with worry as I realised I'd single-handedly moved wardrobes that were much heavier than this one scared boy. Alcohol had given purpose and focus to my rage and I shoved him into a post. Once, twice, it was a blur. A wounded snarl from my brother reminded me he was outnumbered.

The other three were a mass of arms, legs and faces on the ground. I picked a head I didn't recognise and swung a foot. The remaining conscious boy cried out as Frank punched his nose. Exhaustion prevented him from doing much damage even though the lad was too frightened to defend himself. It was as if the shock of seeing his immobile friends had poured ice into his body.

With mutual cries, they both fell over, and the lad wriggled from Frank's embrace, turned over, and crawled away. Frank rolled onto his back and laughed. I looked at the inert figures around us and pulled him to his feet.

He had to be supported through the pitch and putt course and the deserted street that led to the chalet park. Fear of the police dragged the last reserves from our bodies.

As we arrived at the car, our ears strained for sirens. There weren't any but there was no way I could sleep there. Miles over the limit, I edged the vehicle onto the Overstrand Road, and we left the scene of our crimes.

Two and a half horrendous hours felt like twenty as I drove home. Every streetlamp and headlight looked like the beam from a waiting police car. None of them were. My brother slept the entire way and only woke as we entered the outskirts of the city.

I turned the radio off to hear him breathing as he was a mass of congealed blood, yet I became glad of the quiet. I sobered up and tried to comprehend the magnitude of what we'd just done.

Was it self-defence? Or had it gone beyond that? I'd lost control and didn't recognise myself. I suspected that the fact it had occurred when I was drunk for the only time in my life was not a coincidence.

'Where are we?' Frank managed as he rubbed his eyes.

'We're back. Five minutes from home.'

'Crazy night.' It was a statement, not a question. Not one that seemed to bother him. He shook his head and tried to roust himself as I manoeuvred the car onto our drive. I was eighteen years old. It felt like I'd doubled in age through a single experience.

'This isn't me, Frank. Never again. Do you understand?'

He nodded but his thoughts were elsewhere. I noticed then too. Even though my watch said 3 a.m., the lights were on at the front of our house. We let ourselves in the back as usual.

I popped my head round my dad's door, forgetting he slept in the lounge. An action I still repeated twenty times a day to check he was fine. His bed was there with his duvet rolled up on top of it. That was weird, so I followed Frank into the lounge. My mum was in front of the fire. The ashtray next to her full. My brother said nothing, just stared.

'Where's Dad?' I finally said after no information was provided.

She turned from the fire and looked at me with dry eyes. 'He's gone, Vincent.'

'To the hospital?'

'To his maker.'

I knelt beside her. The details didn't matter. She pulled me into an embrace.

'It was for the best,' she said. Her whole body was tense; it must have been shock. I glanced behind me.

Frank stayed at the door, his blue eyes piercing into mine.

He repeated her words. 'It was for the best.'

I heard him clump up the stairs, and the tears for this terrible night finally fell.

11

1985 – AGE: 19

Another strange year. The world around me was changing. AIDS, Live Aid, London riots, but it felt like we'd spent it in a bubble together. My father's death affected me the most, but then I got over it quicker than my mum and Frank.

I thought my mum would recover now she was free of what must have been a terrible burden. She didn't. Perhaps it broke her. She ate little and smoked plenty. We tried to get her to rally with trips out. She came but was quiet.

I thought of the old lady from the Hotel De Paris whose husband died and took half of her with him. It was the same, although that lady was happy to enjoy her twilight years whereas my mum seemed to be rushing towards the exit.

Frank started the job on the Perkins Engines production line. He got me one there too. Sometimes we worked next to each other. It was repetitive hard work with almost unlimited overtime. Ideal for our purposes. I didn't want to focus on the past.

There were a few people I recognised from school there too, although nobody talked to me much. I went back to reading. I thought it would be easier to live my life through others' experiences. The days rolled by and I wondered if anything would ever change. Of course, it did; it always does.

On a sunny Thursday morning, Frank arrived at work and resigned. He'd been getting uptight and twitchy for some unknown reason and just said he was moving away. I'd bought a nearly new Ford Fiesta as a runabout, so we watched him pack his few belongings into the old Cortina.

'So you're going to live with Billy?'

'Yes.'

'Where does Billy live?'

'Not Cromer.'

I flinched.

'Don't worry, they'll never catch us for that.'

'We'd like to know where you are, so we can think of you.' Luckily, my mum appeared to have selective hearing.

'Up north.'

'Up north where?'

'Relax, Mum. I'll write.'

They didn't appear as comfortable with each other since my dad died. Almost as if his absence meant they had to focus on each other, and neither was quite sure how to proceed. He turned to me and shook my hand.

'Vinnie. Good luck.'

He got in the car, honked his horn and, just like that, he left.

My mum put my arm around her as we watched the puff of smoke from the old car dissipate. There was a slight screech of tyres at the end of the road and then he disappeared from view. We both smiled at the sound.

'That was abrupt.'

'Yes, it's a strange world, Vincent.'

'One that I don't understand.'

'Family is all you need in this world, Vincent.'

'Really? We don't seem to have much of ours remaining.' I regretted the words as soon as they were released. They hurt her and I didn't gain anything by saying them.

'We all make mistakes. Then you pay for them. But you do what has to be done.'

'Sometimes I feel like a caged bird. You know, when someone has accidentally left the door open. I hop out and it all looks so mad. So, even though I'm free to do what I like, I still go back in and choose the prison I understand.'

'You'll be fine with me. Don't worry about your brother either. He can look after himself and he'll be home soon. You wait and see.'

'You've been brilliant, you know, Mum. It was you by Dad's side all those years. Frank always talks about it. We're very proud of you.'

She grinned. I wondered later if that was the last time I would think of her as truly happy. She spoke with a lightness that animated her entire face.

'In the end, the only judgement that matters is that of your children.'

We went back inside the house. Just the two of us.

12

1986 – AGE: 20

My mum died late on a Sunday morning. I went to her room because she hadn't got out of bed. I asked her if she wanted a cup of tea and she looked at me and said, 'You're a good boy, Vincent.' As the door closed, I heard a slow sighing sound.

I didn't think too much of it at the time. She produced plenty of strange gasps by that point. I don't believe in souls and such-like but I swear when I left that room it had someone else in it and when I returned with two cups in hand, it was empty. There was, however, a small body with a white face, as if she'd always been made of stone. The cigarette between her fingers had a long line of ash.

I thought about CPR or ringing an ambulance. Not knowing how to do the former and not having a telephone line to do the latter didn't help, but neither were important. It was obvious it was already too late for both. Besides, my mother would have hated an undignified end, being electrocuted or pummelled. Instead, I held her hand and we sat together. It's a strange thing to lose a parent. It's even worse when the second one departs. It's cataclysmic when you have nobody to tell.

I was alone. I looked out of the window and saw a frightening place. Somewhere I would have to venture on my own. There was nobody in my life to talk to at the day's end. Could I overcome my fears? I searched my mind for the strength to begin again, and nothing appeared.

How does a life end where no one needs to be told? Frank hadn't written and he could have been dead for all we knew. After a few hours, her cool skin became cold and stiff. With relief, I remembered our neighbours.

May came back with me and, despite not looking much healthier than my mum, took over. She tried to close Mum's eyes.

'You need to shut them straight away in future, Vinnie.'

'God, sorry. I didn't know.'

'Why would you? You will do next time. Don't worry, your mother isn't bothered now.'

May told me my mum had seen the doctor the previous week. I wasn't aware of that either. He had been wanting her to go for tests for ages but she'd refused. I found the telephone number and rang him from the phone box. He didn't take long. A brisk shake of my hand and a nod and he left me standing at the door. He knew his way to her room. He said, 'She was a strong woman with a weak heart,' and gave us a certificate.

'Put the kettle on, Vinnie,' May said.

'Now what? Do we ring an ambulance?'

'I don't fancy their chances with this one, do you?'

I didn't know what I was expecting from death. Black humour wasn't part of it, but it helped. I'd missed the process for my father and it had never occurred to me to ask.

'Go and get the envelope on my fireplace. Call the funeral parlour. It's all arranged. They'll come for your mum.'

I took another long look at the deceased. The body had diminished in a few short hours. She didn't look peaceful, although it was just like her to have sorted all this beforehand. I couldn't believe that I never knew how ill she was. Maybe there could have been help, but she'd chosen not to take it. Was I not enough to hang on for?

'Make the call. There will be plenty of time for thinking, Vinnie.'

Later, May told me that the pair of them had funeral plans, her and my mum. It was a weird thing to pay for when we had little for living expenses. They both had the minimum cover possible though. The parlour knew what they were dealing with and we got the basics. We'd get the cheapest coffin and no transport. The keen neighbour, Owen, drove us there in the end.

I was nervous as I walked into the crematorium chapel. I felt bad that I had so few people to invite to the funeral. May had told me to take out an advert in the local paper. 'Word gets around,' was what she'd said. I thought what she was implying was that old people read the obituaries. Another 'May' saying.

However, I would have been lost without her. The vicar was there to greet us. I'd explained to May my mother wasn't religious. May said she knew that, but if she was helping, we would do it her way. As she'd said earlier, my mum was beyond caring.

In total, there were ten people present, including the cleric. May, Owen and I sat at the front. Four others huddled together on the row behind. They all looked vaguely familiar, co-workers most likely. An old couple came in as the service started and stayed at the back of the church. There were a lot of empty pews between us, and I wondered if they had just got there early for the next one.

I remembered the endless hours spent at the kitchen table with Mum encouraging me to read after the accident. Her laughing as she shouted out, 'More sandwiches,' to my dad, and,

'Tea, Frank. More tea.' She never let me give up. Sometimes she would fall asleep as I talked.

The service was quick. 'Half-hour slots,' May whispered as she noticed my surprised face. There weren't any eulogies like in the movies. Not for us anyway. I suspected hymns were extra as they were missing too. The vicar didn't know her so his words could have been about anyone who had children and little money. At the end, the coffin moved through a curtain.

> 'We have entrusted our sister to God's merciful
> keeping,
> and we now commit her body to be cremated,
> ashes to ashes, dust to dust,
> in sure and certain hope of the resurrection to
> eternal life,
> through our Lord Jesus Christ,
> who died, was buried, and rose again for us.
> To him be glory for ever. Amen.'

I didn't have any tears in that strange place. None of it felt real, or familiar. I found my mind wandering through the past, and chastised myself for the lack of focus and therefore respect. It was impossible to stop myself doing it though. Maybe everyone considers their lives when they are confronted by their own mortality. I was distracted by the realisation that my parents had led an unusual existence together. No family had come to visit in life or in death. Few friends had made appearances at either funeral. There were just a smattering of work colleagues and May.

'Go to the door, Vinnie. Thank people for coming. Invite them back to the house.'

The four colleagues left quickly with apologies about going so soon. Owen also said he had to return to work although he would drop us off. He held my hand in both of his as he shook it.

'I tried to get through to her. I wasn't enough.'

As he shuffled away, I realised that it was the actions we didn't take that often did the most damage. Her blank stares when he'd offered his company would be buried with him when the time came.

While May talked to the vicar at the front, the old couple who had stayed at the back tried to walk past without saying goodbye.

'Thank you for being here.'

The lady stopped and regarded me with rheumy tearful eyes. One was so milky she couldn't possibly have seen out of it. His face was damp with tears.

'We wanted to make sure that evil woman was dead.'

'Now then, love. That won't help. It's not his fault,' the man said.

He hustled her away. I wondered for a few moments what that was about and then decided that I didn't care. I wanted my mother to take her darkest secrets to the grave. May finally came out and told me that the vicar had declined our invite too.

'Come on, Vinnie. We've got a lot of sandwiches to eat.'

I knocked on May's door first thing the next day, my breath steaming in the chill morning air. I'd been to the shop to get the paper for her. She'd told me the night before, on her fifth sandwich and most of the gin she'd brought over, she hadn't read it in ages as she didn't think she could walk all that way. She used to look forward to the paper, she'd said. My nose had been so stuck in books that I'd missed what was happening right under it. What kind of person was I?

There was no answer so I let myself in with the spare key, which she kept in the pocket of a pinafore hung in the shed. I couldn't recall the last time I'd been inside her house. It was as cold within as out, with a stillness to it that made me nervous. The dog watched me with mournful eyes.

I found her at the bottom of the stairs. White like my mother, yet her face was turned up, with barely a line on it. My mother was in her early fifties, May nearly ninety. Both died exhausted, but only one defeated.

13

1988 – AGE: 22

The council let me stay in the house despite it being in my mum's name. I explained that both Frank and I lived there. It was lucky that he didn't have to sign a form as he still hadn't surfaced or written. The year following the two deaths was weird. When I looked back later, I wondered what I did for all that time. I became a robot, going through the motions. Work, home, eat and occasionally sleep. I felt afraid to engage with a harsh world.

The changes began at work, and I started to emerge; a butterfly from its cocoon. The cruel situations I expected to crush my satin wings didn't exist. Months passed, and I found myself having a laugh with my colleagues. I no longer sat alone at the canteen. They even asked me if I was interested in a promotion. It was flattering to be considered but I still took small steps.

May's funeral was more depressing than my mum's. Not for the fact there were about the same amount of people there, but in my withdrawn state I had failed to notice how lonely she must have been. No one came to my mum's funeral as she wouldn't connect with anyone. Everything she wanted and needed was at home. May lived alone. No wonder her bread was mouldy. It would have taken her two weeks to peck through a loaf.

Owen drove me there again. Poor chap ended up with the dog. He explained the reason for the low attendance was that all her friends and relatives were already dead. Her husband died over twenty years ago, their only child still missing from the Second World War.

I knew none of it. It was the last fact that made me loathe myself more than anything. However, it unearthed a need to rejoin life. May taught me to do my best and face things head on. I was afraid, but at least I began to try. I didn't like to think I was motivated by the desire not to have empty pews when I took my final bow.

Thoughts of Sara came often. I can't now remember whether I burned through that week in the slipstream of her comet, or for the first time I flew myself. Even after I had experienced life at its harshest, I clung to the confidence she gave me. Needless to say, there hadn't been any more girls. Apart from the odd checkout girl and a few office types from work, I'm not sure I'd spoken to any.

Co-workers invited me out after a while. First to pubs, which I declined. Then to cinemas and restaurants, which I attended. That drunken night in Cromer sent a shiver through me whenever it came to mind. It certainly put me off alcohol.

I sometimes imagined it would be nice to go for a walk there. I knew I would have one eye out for Sara, even after all this time, but I could have still enjoyed the memories of the things we had done. Perhaps it would be bittersweet. A kind of pleasant torture. I didn't visit. Knowing my luck there would be 'wanted' posters up with my face on them.

A man at work seemed particularly keen to get me involved in the factory social circle. Oddly, Scott was one from my year at school who had been less than friendly. Maybe he wanted to make up for it. Whatever the reasons were, I took any assistance offered.

Scott said to come bowling with them. He belonged to a league and they were always looking for players. I hadn't played before, but he assured me it was easy. We both laughed at that but the new me needed to give it a go. Scott couldn't drive so the old me wondered if he just wanted a lift. I needed to have more faith in myself.

The night of my first game was a torturous experience. I hadn't thought to ask what people wore for bowling. I couldn't focus on reading and ended up pacing the house. The doorbell distracted me from wistful thoughts of my time with Sara.

I was glad Scott was early as it was evident, even to me, that I needed new memories. I took a deep breath and went to let him in. A shifty woman of about fifty waited at the door. She had an official-looking coat, yet she had the stilted actions of someone uncomfortable with strangers.

'Hello,' she said, after a strange minute as she peered behind me. 'Is your mother in?'

I explained she'd died some time ago.

'I'm sorry to hear that.' She wasn't. Something else dominated her mind and commanded all her attention. 'Is Frank there?'

'Not at the moment,' I said, thinking she didn't look like she was from the council. 'Can I help?'

'I'm looking for Billy. I'm his mum.' At the mention of his name she was fighting tears.

'Didn't he move up north somewhere?'

'We can't find him. We've looked all over.' She sagged at the knees with a sob, so I helped her into the lounge.

After a cup of tea, she composed herself and explained.

'He said he was going away for a bit. To York. He said there was work. Billy had some issues, I'm sure you remember. Not a bad lad, you understand, just boisterous. Anyway. He never rang or wrote. It's been two years now. That's too long. His father and me split up, so it's tough. He's been to York to search but found no trace. I don't even know where to start looking. The police aren't interested. He's twenty-four so he can do what he likes.'

I tried to connect Billy and 'good lad'. It wasn't easy. He was a bully, through and through. He'd just met someone more powerful than him in Frank, and was happy to go along with whatever mischievousness he was led to. I had little to tell her. He and Frank could be anywhere and were more than likely up to no good.

'I'm sure he's fine. You remember what boys are like. He'll be having a great laugh, working hard and playing the same way. Billy's probably lost track of time. I bet they'll be in touch soon.'

'You think? I hope so. We really miss him.'

I must have sounded more convincing than I felt. I didn't want to tell anyone Frank was missing. However, I couldn't imagine she would grass me up to the housing office even if she knew. I also saw it would be reassuring. It reminded me of my mum's placating words when Frank first disappeared. Lies, of course, but helpful back then.

'Frank left a while back and said he was going to live with Billy. I'm sure they'll look out for each other.'

She flinched at the mention of his name.

'When was that?'

'Less than a year ago.' It wasn't, nearer two. At least she would think they were both alive and well at that point in time.

She aged in front of me and couldn't get away quick enough. I offered to give her a lift home as Scott arrived, but she tottered off without replying.

'Who was that?' Scott said.

'Billy's mum, you know, Frank's mate from school.'

'That nutter. What did she want?'

'She hasn't seen him for a while.'

'Probably for the best. He and Frank were trouble.'

'Were they that bad?'

Scott thought hard before he answered.

'I understand he was family, Vinnie. But there was something missing from both those two.' After another pause, he continued. 'Frank was your brother and I accept he was sticking up for you, but he scared a lot of folk. We were all just having a laugh, but some of the stuff he said and did to people was evil.'

As I locked the door behind me, I wondered whether he understood how hurtful 'just having a laugh' could be. It hadn't been fun for me and the others that had been the butt of their jokes. Did any of us examine our actions accurately? I liked to think he'd recognised the consequences of his actions and he'd changed. Maybe my brother and his kind were the only thing that had stopped Scott and his friends going too far.

'What did they do that was so wrong?'

'The rumour is that he killed that boy who bullied you after you deliberately trod on his foot in the queue. You must remember the one. He used to celebrate scoring for the school team by shouting "Victory" at the top of his voice.'

'What? I didn't do it deliberately. It was an accident. And he drowned, which had nothing to do with Frank either. That's all rubbish.'

'Yeah, I heard he was knocked out before he fell in.'

Did I remember it wrong? It was possible as I wouldn't have been paying attention.

'Frank wouldn't do that. It was an accident.'

'Sure. It was ages ago anyway. Come on, let's go. We've got a game to win.'

I didn't know what Frank was capable of, not really, but I couldn't see him as a killer. He'd protected me more than I'd thought though. Could I judge him? There were different kinds of wrong. Some were worse than others. I would have many years to focus on that fact.

14

1989 – AGE: 23

My brother finally came home at 3 a.m. on a Wednesday in early October. I remembered the time because he woke me up by hammering on the front door. At first, I thought it was the police and lay cowering in my bed. It was at times like these that I envied psychopaths. Their complete lack of conscience, empathy, remorse, guilt or shame must allow them refreshing sleep. I wondered if they still felt fear.

It was only when I heard him shout through the letterbox, 'For God's sake, Vinnie,' that I got up. He slid into the house like a desperate fox after a lengthy hunt. In close proximity, he smelt the same too.

Frank never carried much weight but he looked undernourished, even from the fleeting glance I gave him as he skirted by. He disappeared upstairs, went into his old room and that was it. It was as though he were fourteen again.

He came downstairs late in the afternoon and ate like a man who'd discovered food for the first time. I sat opposite, watched, and waited. He had scratches on his face and had clearly been in a fight. If he'd won, the loser would've suffered. In the end, I don't think he would have talked at all if I hadn't pressed.

'Where you been, Frank?'

'All over.'

'You know Mum's gone?'

'I heard.'

'That's it? You missed her funeral.'

'I'm aware of that. I found out late.'

'Not too late to get in touch.'

'It's been tough, Vinnie. There's been some nasty things happen.'

'You going to explain?'

'No. I did what needed to be done.'

That phrase again. I dreaded to think what undercurrents lurked under that benign expression.

'Where's Billy, Frank?'

'He's disappeared.'

He carried on eating in silence, avoiding my stare.

'I have to go. I'll be in touch.'

With no further comment, he vanished again. I felt like rubbing my eyes to make sure I hadn't imagined it. It became obvious to me I had no one in my corner. To live life, you had to talk to someone and share your fears and concerns. I resolved then to let that happen. Part of me had been waiting for Frank to return so I could start again. I could see that now for the pointless exercise it always was.

As for Billy, that was worrying. Frank said he'd disappeared. Not 'gone', or 'I have no idea where he is'. What could I do? I didn't fancy going to visit his mother. I did what most people had to do at times like these – nothing.

15

1990 – AGE: 24

Events developed for me as the weather took a turn for the better. I'd always loved spring. You got to the end of winter and just when you thought it was going to be cold, damp and dark forever, life changed. Then, you were pleasantly surprised. As for most people, the good things in life happened when I least expected them.

My boss interrupted me on the production line. I had ear protectors on, so he tapped me on the back to get my attention.

'Vinnie, Personnel want to see you.'

To my workmates' amusement, he did so as an alarm sounded and the conveyor belt stopped. I suspect the people in their houses a few miles from the factory heard him too. I had to walk the length of the factory to cheers and jibes from every man there.

It was light-hearted and in good humour, but it reminded me of school. The dreaded procession through the playground with abuse hurled from every angle. Even the nice kids turned their heads so as not to be associated with me. By the time I got to the offices I was shaking.

The only person I had talked to about feeling like this was Sara. I didn't have an inkling what they wanted me for, therefore my mind searched for the darkest possible reason. Sara had told me I was a gentle soul. She'd said everyone feels similar at times. Instead, try imagining a positive outcome. Or failing that, think of something else. What you are having for tea, for example.

I tried conjuring up pay rises and promotions, iced buns and milkshakes. I entered the bright shiny world of the offices upstairs expecting to be, at best, sacked on the spot, and at worst, cuffed, stripped naked and thrown into a meat wagon for crimes against children and puppies.

I never felt comfortable up there. The women seemed impossibly glamorous. High heels and short tight skirts abounded, with make-up so thick I couldn't imagine what they looked like underneath. I wasn't sure who they were trying to impress as I'd only ever seen one man working with them. He seemed too showy to be interested in bright red lipstick and smoky eye shadow. Unless he was putting it on himself. He looked the safest bet so it was him I approached.

'Vincent Roach, for Personnel.'

'Pardon, speak up, please.'

I self-consciously repeated myself, a little louder.

'Who wants Vincent Roach?' he sang, as though he were checking who had ordered the soup of the day.

'Clara does. She's doing the DISs.'

'Ah, another victim for the new girl. Far corner, Mr Roach. Next to the window.'

I wandered over, my mind trying to solve the abbreviation. I tried not to think of dismissal, or disaster, or even dismemberment, but it proved impossible. The desk looked empty. Just as I approached, a round face with curly blonde hair popped up from behind a partition. She gave me a sweet smile and told me to sit down on the seat next to her.

'Morning, Vincent. How are you?'

'Fine, good. Um, and you?'

'Hungry. It's only eleven but my stomach thinks it's two.'

I was unsure what to say to that. She seemed wired. Maybe she wanted my packed lunch. One of her eyes was just a little off kilter. I found it very hard to decide which to look at, and my gaze flicked from one to the other. It made her appear both cute and vulnerable. I decided to focus at the lower centre of her forehead before she thought me insane too.

'I know you, don't I?' she said.

'Do you?'

'Yes, from the bowling alley. I was there on Sunday, five lanes up from you. My name's Clara. You got four strikes in a row with the first four balls. We all stopped, in case you hit the fifth one.'

'I don't pay much attention to what's happening around me.'

I said it deadpan, so I did indeed sound bonkers. Very smooth. If she wasn't going to sack me before, she would wish she could after that.

'Ah, okay. Well, you should say hello next time. I don't know many people there and it's always nice to pretend I have friends.'

She smiled but there was a hint of truth in the joke.

'I will do.'

'Great. That made me sound sad.' She emitted a high-pitched laugh after she spoke. I noticed she was as nervous as I was.

'Anyway, we're updating the Death In Service beneficiaries and you haven't replied to our letters. You have your mother on the form at the moment, but I understand she passed away.'

DIS – Death In Service. I laughed out loud, which surprised us both. I remembered the correspondence they'd sent; in fact, I could see the letter in my mind on the table by the door. I wondered how she knew my mum was dead. Although I supposed it wasn't a secret.

'Yes, I'm sorry. I kept forgetting.'

'Who would you like to put? We can do the paperwork here.'

I looked up at the ceiling as I considered my options. It didn't take long. Short of giving it to a charity, that only left my wayward brother.

'Frank,' I said. 'Frank Roach, my brother.'

I signed the bottom of the form and stood to leave.

'See you at bowling, Vincent.'

'Definitely, we'll talk then.'

After five paces, I turned to have another look. I had an unusual urge to know if she wanted to go to dinner with me. She could have what she liked out of my lunch box. She had answered her phone by then and was talking to the caller. I could see her querying a small compact mirror and rubbing her forehead with a frown. I decided to leave while I was still ahead.

16

1991 – AGE: 25

Unusually, the company Christmas party happened in early January. There had been some kind of administrative balls-up and, due to the size of the workforce, they could only find a place with the capacity after the new year. I'd never been to one before.

The stories I'd heard were enough to put me off. It was strange, but the drunken shenanigans seemed to be almost a badge of honour amongst the production staff. The thought of letting myself down somehow and having to arrive on Monday morning to judging stares made me sweat with dread. However, this time, Clara was going.

The suspicion she liked me had been confirmed tenfold by the fact she found it necessary to come down to the factory floor. I'd not seen her there before. Yet I would find her smiley face behind me on regular occasions. Much to the amusement of my friends. It seems strange saying that, but I'd become a popular guy.

It appeared me and bowling were like peas and carrots. I wasn't sure why we clicked – maybe it was focus. Someone showed me how to hook the ball and I did it first time. I learnt fast and became the best in the team and had the third highest average in the league. I was still the same person, but success made me welcome.

My simple qualities of reliability, soberness and consistency were respected and admired. At school, they were weaknesses – things to be ridiculed. Clara was there every week. I even picked her up in my car a few times.

We were awkward around each other, with occasional long silences that both of us struggled to break. Other moments we laughed, often over nothing. When we said our goodbyes, I could see her battling with what she wanted to say but never did. I hoped to ask her for a date too. We were like boxers circling in the ring in the first round. I wasn't worried as even I could tell contact was inevitable.

I offered to pick Clara up for the party but she said she would meet me there. I was all of a jitter beforehand and decided to walk to the hotel, even though it would take nearly an hour. As per usual, I had stupid worrying thoughts about there not being any parking spaces or my car breaking down on the way.

It was a clear night and my breath steamed in front of me. I couldn't decide if I was nervous because it would be a room full of strangers – I generally was in social situations – or if it was because I hoped things would happen between us. The physical activity helped and I spent the journey inventing topics to discuss. There were people everywhere when I arrived, and the crowd outside was already in high spirits. More than a few seemed to have made a head start on the booze. I took a quiet moment and walked in.

My throat tickled from the march, so I looked for somewhere to get a drink and made my way through the throng. Having purchased new clothes, I strode in, hoping to disguise my nervousness. I'd found that if you bought nice outfits, many people didn't see past them to the person inside. The bar area heaved with enthusiastic drinkers and was unappealing.

'Vincent, glad you came.' Scott ambled over and beamed at me.

'Hiya, busy, isn't it?'

'Sure is. We'll be getting stuck into the office totty later. Best we get some Dutch courage in us. What do you want?'

'I'll get the first one, mate.'

He shouted 'lager' at me with a toothy grin. I sneaked a quick peek to see if Clara had arrived and he laughed. I'd have made a poor spy.

'Looking for anyone in particular?'

'Just checking to see if your mum's turned up.'

He roared with amusement and sprayed me with the remnants of his current drink. I'd shocked myself. When did I become so cheeky?

The barman served me quicker than I expected. That was more energy wasted fretting over something that never happened. I'd had a weird nightmare a few days before where I imagined standing at the bar for hours as everyone else got served before me. When I returned to Clara, she was being successfully chatted up by George Clooney. He then proceeded to take both drinks off me and put a ten-pound note in my top jacket pocket.

I gave Scott a lifeless lager and sipped my bottle of Kaliber. It was the first alcoholic drink I'd had in ages, even if it only registered 0.5 per cent strength. I placed my hand over the label to fool would-be mickey takers. It tasted like it had been filtered through a pair of dirty underpants. However, the grimace dropped from my face the moment I saw Clara walk in.

It felt like looking at a relative of the Clara I knew. She wore more make-up than usual and a blue dress with frills to her knees. The halter-neck top was struggling to contain her cleavage. If you wanted to be cruel, you could have described Clara as short and fat. She wasn't much over five feet tall. She had strong arms too, maybe from all the bowling; her ball weighed the same as mine and she bowled hard.

I thought of her as comely, more pocket rocket than flighty deer. I realised her shape was similar to Sara's. Perhaps I had a type. The crowd cleared for a moment and I noticed her high heels and calves. She looked simply beautiful. My skin shrank as she teetered towards me.

Standing next to me, she wasn't much shorter than I was. It was a little unsettling and my mouth filled with saliva.

'You got here, then?'

Scott, who was still beside me, exploded with laughter.

'I'll catch you lovebirds later.'

Clara looked up at me and I felt her hand take mine and squeeze. 'Yes, I appear to have managed that. A drink would be nice.'

I grinned too and knew the night would be special.

Annoyingly, and typically, it took ages to get served. I even sneaked a look back to make sure that git, Clooney, hadn't made his move.

I got her the pint of Foster's she asked for and one for myself too. A few long sips lubricated my tongue and soon we were having fun. The party passed in a blur. We spent the whole evening together, gliding round the room and chatting to different groups.

She professed to not being much of a drinker either and we moved on to Cokes or lime and sodas. When it was just me and her, we giggled and occasionally flesh met. Just a brush of the arm, or a fleeting touch. Near the end of the night, they played a few love songs and dancers became pairs and smooched.

'Let's dance?' I said.

'I don't dance much. I don't think I'm very good at it.'

'Neither am I.'

'Won't we look like arseholes, then?'

We chuckled like children at that.

'It'll be fun. No one's looking at us.'

'That's what my mum used to say when I was young and didn't want to get changed on the beach. I'm sure she was wrong about that too.'

Her eyes were wide and her fear genuine.

'Come on, Clara.'

I put my hand behind her back and guided her towards the dance floor. We sought the safety of the centre. She fitted into my arms like she belonged there and, with increasing confidence, we moved in unison. It was more rocking from side to side than anything else. I couldn't help but recall the muscular movements Sara used to make.

As we relaxed into it, I was aware of a light pressure on my bum. Then Scott laughed as he skated past with the director's PA and out of sight. Then the weight was returned and Clara placed her face close to mine. When we kissed, the room disappeared and we were on our own. It had been a perfect night.

It was strange how I'd always worried about upcoming events. Those sleepless nights trying to play through every scenario and eventuality were pointless. Taking a risk could lead to the best of things. So it was with me.

17

1992 – AGE: 26

I'd never been a big fan of politics, but even I'd heard of Margaret Thatcher letting people buy their own council house. It seemed everyone was at it, so I became involved too. It was a complicated and stressful procedure. I kept thinking something would go wrong. It didn't and, why would it? It wasn't like there was a chain and I wasn't actually moving.

Any break from the norm seemed to trigger anxiety in me. This time, though, I had Clara to share the experience with. She didn't know what she was doing either, but we got through it together.

She came one afternoon to celebrate 'completion', as the solicitor called it. I'd adopted a weird habit since the day before when I'd received the confirmation letter. I'd taken to walking through the rooms and marvelling at the fact I owned everything. With the discount they gave me, I was able to clear the balance – just over twenty thousand – with my savings. Peterborough's housing market was way off London's levels and it wasn't like I lived in a desirable part either.

There was still a fair amount of money left too. Scott said I worked hard and played light. Clara was the same. We were having a Chinese tonight. She loved takeaways, and that was as extravagant as she got. She treated me then, even though she earned less than half what I did.

Our relationship was like an icebreaker on an Arctic sea. Steady, consistent and reliable. We'd get to our destination at our own speed. We had sex for the first time about three months after the party. She insisted on getting steaming drunk and turning out the lights. It was an unusual feeling, being the experienced one. I liked that I was the only man she'd known intimately.

It got better as we relaxed although it was very different from how it was with Sara. I pushed away any thoughts of comparisons with her and our time in Cromer. I knew it wasn't fair. Nine years had gone by, I needed to let go. I couldn't decide if being twenty-six suited me or not. I did know I felt much happier than I had in a long time.

Clara came barrelling through the back door with a sweaty face.

'My Lord, did you get a set meal for five by mistake?'

'The guy in the shop gave me extra for free. You know how he has a soft spot for me.'

Hard spot, more like, but I let it go. I slid the plates out of the oven, where I'd put them to keep warm. Clara laughed her head off the first time I did that, thinking it weird. I wasn't sure what was so funny as she used the microwave to heat her non-microwavable plates up. She spread the food out on the table. Five people was an underestimate. We had a lot of routines like that. We were like a married couple before we'd tied the knot. Before I'd even asked her.

She was in high spirits.

'I can't believe you're a homeowner, Vinnie. That's so exciting.'

'Hard to believe, you mean.'

'No, you work long hours and deserve it. Is having a mortgage scary?'

She wasn't aware of the finer points of my financial situation. I hadn't told her before as I'd worried it would fall through. For a while I wondered if it was because I didn't want her to know. It wasn't though. I wanted to impress her.

'Here's the final paperwork and the monthly payments.'

Clara stared hard at the sheet of paper, Chinese food wedged between her teeth. The chicken ball dropped onto her plate with an unhealthy splodge as the amounts hit home.

'It says balance outstanding zero and monthly payment zero.'

'That's right.'

'You own it outright?'

'Yep, every dusty brick and flaking piece of paint.'

'How?'

'The government paid nearly half and I covered the rest from all the overtime I've done over the years. I didn't even know what I was saving it for.'

'Vinnie, you're so clever. Now you have something that nobody can take away. Yours forever.'

'Ours forever.'

She looked at me with her mouth opening and closing. It wasn't a great look, to be honest, but I was swept along by the emotion and going on one knee seemed to be the most natural thing in the world.

'Will you marry me?'

'Oh my God, of course.'

'I'm sorry, I haven't got a ring.'

'Fuck the ring, Vincent. You've got a house.'

She kissed me with a fervent desire that no amount of alcohol had been able to resurrect so far. I was dragged upstairs so fast I jarred my shoulder on the banister and my knee on numerous steps.

She ripped my T-shirt pulling it over my head. She pushed me onto the bed and she mounted me, eyes boring into mine. I realised the lights were still on as she moaned and slid with an intensity I would never have believed she possessed. It was bloody amazing.

My mind was all over the place, but my body knew its destination. I tried to get her to slow down so my lack of control wouldn't disappoint.

'The food will be cold.'

She gave me a demonic grin.

'We can eat it between sex sessions.'

18

1993 – AGE: 27

My brother's timing, for once, was bad. Yet again, I hadn't heard from him for a long time. He would never be a candidate for letter writer of the year; in fact, I wasn't sure he could write. It was a shame he was so poor at keeping in touch, or, failing that, it was a pity he didn't return a few weeks before he did.

The simple notion that someone wanted to marry her invigorated Clara. It lit a fire under our bed and gave her a burst of confidence that brought about a startling difference to her normal demeanour. She wasn't a bridezilla as such, but she couldn't stop telling people about it. Then inviting them to the wedding, despite us not having set the date.

She would display the ring we purchased together and then talk. Some of what came out of her mouth was true; however, a lot of it she made up on the spot. Either that or, more likely, she spent most of her waking hours imagining the wonderful life we'd have and just talked about one of those scenarios. I didn't worry too much and assumed she would calm down in time.

She wanted to have children. Lots of them. 'I will be the best housewife and mother in the world,' she would say. Okay, it was a little scary. I would provide for them, amongst other things. I realised that I hadn't thought about what a woman might want from life. Although I hadn't paid my own existence much attention either.

The security of owning a house had given Clara access to her dreams of a perfect married life. As we'd got to know each other I'd found her time at school had been similar to mine. Whereas I'd immersed myself in books, she seemed to have fantasised and created different lives for herself.

That didn't make her crazy, I hoped. Far from it, in fact. Now she was so close to achieving her ideal, she became eminently sensible. The ring cost less than the thick leather jacket she had bought me the previous Christmas. Clara saved money for a rainy day like a squirrel planning for Armageddon.

Despite her inviting total strangers, an extravagant wedding wasn't required, and she was happy to wear a relative's old dress to cut costs. She wasn't superstitious, as Aunt Tessa was killed by a tram in Blackpool. Although I don't think she was wearing the dress at the time.

The problem came from me. I didn't have much understanding of what a wedding involved. I did know I wanted Frank there. He was all the family I had left and would be my best man. He was the only person from my childhood that knew me well. The bit of my childhood I remembered anyway. Having him there would be an anchor to the past so I knew who I was.

Sadly, I didn't know where he lived and had no idea how to reach him. I explained this to Clara and at first she understood. As the months ticked by, she began to get twitchy, as though I were trying to avoid setting a date. Maybe that was why she kept mentioning it to all and sundry, to make sure I wouldn't forget.

She'd never met Frank and thought it strange that I would be so bothered over someone, brother or not, whom I hadn't seen for three years and was so careless at staying in touch. After six months of no contact, I relented, and we set a date for early the following year.

She wanted it all planned beforehand and almost insisted I ask Scott to be my best man. I did – and he agreed, although with less enthusiasm than I hoped. Clara was an only child and her dad maintained he would pay for everything. Thirty-five people we were able to muster. That pleased me, despite a fair number of them being her relatives, but Clara was disappointed. At that point, I decided to stop trying to understand women and let it wash over me.

I finally received a postcard from Leeds and, as it stated, Frank turned up with a fiancée of his own on a hot Sunday in late summer. I told Frank we would cook for him when he arrived. Clara chose to do a roast chicken, and was sweating and panicking in the kitchen.

I was working under my bonnet with a guy called Silent Kevin from work. I suppose we'd become friends, although it was hard to say as he didn't get his nickname for nothing. He worked on the production line too, but his real love was cars. The Ford Fiesta had been playing up and Clara had mentioned spending the money to buy a more family-oriented vehicle, or at least one with four doors. It felt like tempting fate, so Kevin had started coming over a few months back to see if he could sort out the problems.

He always brought four beers with him. One each whilst fixing the car and one each after eating dinner. Clara cooked him something as a thank you. It never seemed to occur to him that she might want a drink. I wasn't sure if he was lonely or not. Whenever I asked him if he wanted to come over, he was usually free. That day, he arrived with only two beers as he had declined the invite to the family reunion afterwards.

'It's no use you hiding under there, you know.'

I pulled myself out from under the engine and there he stood, with the same look on his face. As though the pair of us had been out the night before and got drunk, and he'd popped round at lunchtime to try and tempt me into going for a livener. A good feeling flowed through me. His hair seemed longer with a few flecks of grey, but other than that he looked the same. The lady with him was striking. She had a short red, harsh bob on top of an expressionless face of heavy make-up.

My brother introduced me to Rebel with a squeeze to my shoulder. I got a cool handshake in return. Frank gazed at her with blatant admiration and held her other hand whilst he talked.

'This is my brother, Vincent. The one I told you about. You can call him Vinnie, like I do. Still managing to keep this on the road, are you?'

He gestured to my car. As he did, Kevin came out from underneath it. He glanced at my brother and Rebel, decided nothing interested him and nodded at me.

'I can't get those screws done up. I'm not sure we've put it back in right.'

Before I could speak, Frank cut in.

'Vinnie, you go and introduce Rebel to your missus. I'll give your friend a hand here.'

I looked at my brother and Kevin, then at Rebel, who studied me. None of us were happy with that arrangement. Frank shooed us off, and I took her round the back. She noticed the concrete slope at the back with confusion and seemed relieved when she found Clara wasn't in a wheelchair. Even though I was keen to return to the others, Clara waylaid me with concerns over cooking times. I feared what I might get back to as the other two made an unusual pair.

I needn't have worried. They were laughing together when I returned and drinking beer. Frank put my empty bottle on the pavement and grinned.

'Clever bloke, this. Great man to keep around.'

Kevin beamed like he'd been awarded a prize.

'Frank did it with good, old-fashioned brute force. It was easy after that. I'll have to get his number so he can help out again.'

To my surprise, I felt let down. I couldn't remember the last time he had put three sentences together with me. He picked his toolbox up, smiled, and walked away.

'Isn't he staying for lunch?'

'No, he has another motor to work on.'

'Doesn't he say goodbye?'

'Not often, no.'

'I like him.'

'And my beer by the looks of things.'

'I was just being polite. It tasted like transmission fluid.'

He leaned against the side of the car and yawned.

'What do you think?'

'Yeah, I don't like it either.'

'Not the drink, stupid. Rebel.'

'Very pretty.'

'Isn't she? I'm in love. She's the one for me.'

He laughed at my raised eyebrows.

'Early days though. Let's just say we're having fun.'

'Congratulations.'

'And to you. Surely it's me who's supposed to get married first.'

He was joking, but I needed to tell him the news. I'd left it out of my letter back to him as I wanted to inform him personally. It had been eating me up as the days ticked by.

'Frank, I asked a friend called Scott to be the best man.'

He actually recoiled. I took a step towards him and he waved me away.

'That's fine, Vinnie. I'm aware I haven't been around. I didn't know where the time vanished to start with. I looked all over for work. It was a struggle without qualifications. Then I found out about Mum's family.'

Now it was I who reacted.

'I thought her parents were dead, and she was an only child.'

'She was an only child and her parents are dead, but, Vinnie, they only died five years ago.'

It's hard to say what passed through my brain over the next few seconds. Lots of the books I read told of the special relationships between grandparents and grandchildren. I'd had many a thought as to how grounding that would have been. Why were we denied this?

'I did meet a few cousins though.'

'Will they want to come to the wedding?'

'I wouldn't have thought so,' he said with a sad smile.

'Why didn't we know them?'

'They disowned Mum, years ago. Look, it's all in the past now. There isn't any point in raking up what's been left behind. I wasn't sure what to tell you and that was part of why I didn't come back. Then I met Rebel, and I really did forget everyone else. Now, come on. Mum told me to watch out for you after she was gone. Who is this best man?'

'It's Scott, from your year at school.'

'What?' His rage was instant. 'That fucking prick.'

The meal didn't go too well. Frank had brought two bottles of wine, which I think helped him forget the best man news as he drank most of them himself. Clara was clumsy with everything and said little. I wondered if she was intimidated by Rebel's beauty or my brother's silence. Rebel's tight clothes showed off an admirably slim figure, which Frank didn't seem able to resist touching. Their interaction was unusual, with an edge to it. She watched him like an observer of a street fight. Some girls loved danger.

They made me remember the time Frank and I put an aerosol canister on a bonfire. As the fire licked the sides of it, a tinging sound came out. This got louder and faster until we both began to step away, unsure as to what might happen. With an almighty bang, it blasted fifty feet up in the air and blew wood and burning plastic over our crouching heads. All that remained was a smouldering patch on the ground. I feared something similar might occur here. By the time dessert had disappeared, it was a relief to get them out of my house.

19

1994 – AGE: 28

Scott insisted I have a stag do. He also asserted that it would be a pub crawl. The dreaded – or loved, depending on your drinking habits – 'Crown to Town'. Fifteen, mostly grotty, pubs along Lincoln Road with a pint in each place. For someone who drank it was no small task, for someone who didn't it was mountainous. The sensation I got as I looked at the creaking sign for The Crown was one of an inexperienced climber gaping up at Everest. The only concession he would allow was you could have a spirit at every third pub. He said that would avoid bloating.

There were seven of us in all. My brother had returned to Leeds and stayed in touch. However, he didn't confirm whether he would come for the pub crawl, just that they would be there on the day. Scott and I assumed he would be absent.

When Frank rocked up at the pub a little after 6.30 p.m. and saw us gathered at the bar in our matching bright white Magnificent Seven T-shirts, it was a bad sign. The seven were me, Silent Kevin, Scott, twins called Arthur and Alan who were nice quiet guys from work and my bowling team, and a couple of Scott's friends from work. I knew their faces, little else, but Scott assured me it was the more, the merrier. He would be wrong.

With Frank there, we became the hateful eight. In hindsight, the look that passed between Scott and Frank as he arrived should have been enough to get me to ring a taxi, go home, and put it down to a poor idea. Less blood would have been spilt too.

The first four pubs weren't too bad. My nervousness gave me a dry mouth, and the beer actually helped calm me down. Everyone seemed to be getting on well and talking about man things. I saw my brother chatting to Kevin with great gusto. Scott and I even fitted a quick pool game in at The Windmill against Alan and Arthur.

Nevertheless, the ferocious pace needed to grace the final pub before closing was too much for a lightweight such as me, and I began to flag. After we left the eleventh pub, I waddled down the street like an overfilled rain barrel on bowed legs.

Despite a considerable amount of boasting from Scott and his friends about what massive drinkers they were, all three of them were worse for wear. Scott's voice became progressively louder and more obnoxious with every watering hole we visited. This, combined with the congratulatory braying by the two friends at his rubbish jokes, began to get us disapproving looks from everyone in our vicinity. The barman at The Hand and Heart asked us to finish our drinks and leave.

Soon enough, it wasn't fun any more. It started to feel like we were prisoners of war being marched at punishing speed by an evil officer – Scott, in our case. As we trudged to The Norfolk, Alan and Arthur lagged behind. I dropped back to see if they were okay.

'How's it going, lads? Almost there.'

They both looked apologetic but steadfast.

'We've had enough, Vinnie. We don't drink much and certainly not at this pace. I'm so full I can hardly breathe.'

For a few seconds, I thought about trying to persuade them to stay. In reality, I wanted to leave with them.

'We've both got work tomorrow too.'

They shook my hand and disappeared. The empty street seemed darker. The speed they left was indicative of the fact they were probably worried Scott would come back and shoot them at the roadside for not keeping up.

I was stepping through the doorway into the next pub when I remembered the factory was shut on Sunday for maintenance.

The atmosphere had taken a turn for the worse when I stood at the bar with the remaining participants. Frank and Scott squared up to each other. Scott's mates were behind him in threatening poses. Silent Kevin seemed oblivious to the quarrel as he got served.

'Heh, what's going on?' I said.

'This guy is a dick. You sure you want him as your best man?'

'You're just jealous that he asked me.'

'Not jealous, just surprised.'

Kevin came and stood between them as he handed out the drinks. This seemed to defuse the tension, although more alcohol would not improve the atmosphere of violence that hung around us. Scott's trio went to play the fruit machine and left us staring at each other.

'What was that about, Frank?'

'I'm sorry, Vinnie. I overheard something and challenged him. He didn't like it and got all shirty. He always was a bully.'

'Can't you forget it, please? We only have a few more pubs and then it's over.'

Frank's expression told me I was incorrect.

'Where are the other two?' said Kevin, noticing the absence of the twins.

'They escaped.'

It kicked off at the Harvester. By this time, I was seeing double and struggling to keep any tension in my face. The thought of more liquid was an awful prospect. Kevin and I had dropped to the rear.

When we got to the car park, we were met by a tangle of four bodies rolling around in the dirt. It was a dark night and difficult to see what was happening. There were only a few spaces with cars in as it was more a food pub than a boozer. By 10.30 p.m., it seemed everyone had eaten and gone home so there was no one to raise the alarm.

One of Scott's friends rolled from the melee and lay on the floor, half conscious. It was hard to tell if he was paralytic or injured. The other two were getting the better of Frank. Scott was a sturdy man now and his friend similar. It was a vicious fight, not a fair one, with fists and boots being rained down at every opportunity.

I looked about for a stick or stone. Anything to even the sides. The single streetlight was no help. I felt desperate as the grey fog of alcohol lifted to reveal a red mist of rage. I grabbed Scott's remaining friend by the back of his coat and threw him away from the fight. He turned and came at us, but Kevin stood in the way and he put his hands up, saying, 'Okay, that's enough.'

Meanwhile, Scott had pulled a small knife on Frank and had him backed up against a wall. Scott lunged at him. Frank grabbed the arm that was holding the knife and pushed it skyward. As I ran towards them, I saw a piece of dislodged tarmac and scooped it up. Using two hands and with all the force my fury could muster, I bashed it on the back of Scott's skull. The lump broke in half as Scott slumped to his knees. With each piece as a weapon, I pounded the top of his head with the sharp edges as though I were a drummer at the crescendo of an ancient sacrifice.

Strong arms lifted me away from the scene.

'Steady now. You've won,' Kevin said.

Scott rolled onto his back and let out a painful cry. The friend I had pulled away came to his assistance and looked down in shock. Turning to me, with hate in his eyes, he snarled his response.

'You lunatic. You could have killed him. I'm ringing the police.'

Scott's bloodied hand rose up, and he managed to gurgle, 'No.'

'He's right. Vinnie did what had to be done defending me. Scott here brought a knife to the party,' Frank said.

The man thought for a minute and nodded.

'Fuck off, then. I'll ring for an ambulance, say we were mugged by kids or something.'

Kevin hailed a passing black cab and we got into the back. The gloom was a good thing as my hands were sticky with blood. Frank managed a smile.

'Sorry, Vinnie. I keep getting you into trouble.'

All I could think was at least Scott wouldn't mind not being my best man.

The wedding happened three weeks later. I suppose you could say it was a success, comparatively anyway. There were no-shows. Scott was one, and Frank was the other. Neither were surprising. I think, deep down, part of me felt pleased. The chances of any drama decreased.

Alan and Arthur told me Scott was kept in hospital for observation for four days and had been off sick since. His two friends from our pub crawl steered a wide path from me. If I were a certain type of man, I would have found it comical. However, the thought of Scott returning was an unpleasant one. I struggled to relax at work.

It was still depressing to think I had no family present at my wedding. Silent Kevin was best man. He surprised us with a very witty speech. I was lucky to have a friend like him. Alan and Arthur also came. The neighbour, Owen, who liked my mother after my dad passed, also attended. He had slipped from my mind. I see now that it's easy to do. You become so involved in your own life that you neglect others.

Owen had aged disproportionately in the years since those funerals. Not that I knew his age or when his birthday was. He was thrilled to be invited and stood on the groom's side of the church with a grin. He more than paid us back by dancing like a professional and became a big hit on the day.

As I watched his exuberance pull people from their shells, me included, I wondered if life would find a way of punishing me for my neglect. Was it a crime to be lazy and thoughtless?

Clara's dad gave her away. It was the only time I'd seen him show even a glimmer of enthusiasm for anything. I should have taken the warning. I felt bad because as she walked up the aisle, my first thought was that she looked enormous. She'd complained about putting on weight, but I had brushed it aside. It didn't bother me, although her off-the-shoulder wedding dress made me think of rugby prop forwards.

It was a lovely service. I was nervous and kept muddling my words up. Clara, on the other hand, said her piece loud and clear. This was her day and she was going to enjoy it. We went for a nice meal at The Queensgate Hotel after the service and then through to the lounge for a few drinks.

Gradually everyone filtered away and it was just the two of us at the bar. She was flushed with a big smile. Silent Kevin was in a corner living up to his name because the remaining bridesmaid had her tongue down his throat and speech would have been impossible.

'Shall we go up to our room and get up to mischief, my husband?'

The effect of sitting on a bar stool had made her cleavage heave up so it was almost under her chin. Like she was peeking over two speckled space hoppers. That was my good fortune – I'd always considered breast was best. Although, I couldn't help thinking I was staring at one of those colossal breakfasts which were free if you could eat it all. In the spirit of that, I would give it my best shot.

20

1995 – AGE: 29

Popularity, for me at least, was like a sand sculpture on a beach: only to be enjoyed for a short period. After being bullied at school I'd become acutely aware when I was the focus of others' attention. We had our honeymoon straight after the wedding and when I returned to work, the damage was done.

I was back to where I started, yet things were different. For the first time in my life people were scared of me. I recognised my own responses from years ago in the faces of people I spoke to. They didn't know what to say to me as they had concerns about how I would react. As though at any moment I might scream at them.

It was insane. Men I had worked with for years, and barely spoken to, went out of their way to avoid me. Those I sat next to at the canteen would finish their meals in a hurry. Upstairs in the offices, conversations would go quiet as I appeared.

At least Scott only worked there briefly afterwards and avoided me the entire time. Heaven knows what he and his friends had said about me. He soon left for a job at the steelworks up north. Some of the rumours filtered through to the league I played in, yet they were an enduring bunch there and the fact Scott never reappeared helped. I suspect my rising bowling average was also a factor.

Clara seemed oblivious. She had a new focus, and this was all consuming. I'd never spent much time thinking about the future when I battled the present. Life happened and you dealt with things as they occurred. In that respect, I found it hard to understand Clara's obsession. She wanted children. Immediately.

In all aspects of life, that level of inflexibility and desire will cause problems if it isn't resolved or satisfied. The possibility we might not be able to have children, for whatever reason, never entered her focused mind. That aside, we were content for the first six months of our marriage. The issues at work were forgotten as we became very inward-looking. We still saved what we could, for the time when Clara would be off with the kids, and we had lots of sex.

To begin with, I enjoyed it. A whole new side to Clara opened up. Nurses' outfits and role-playing were her favourite way to get me in the mood. Even the pregnancy tests were almost fun. 'Not this time,' she would joke. It became a time to endure. To Clara, nothing else mattered. Emotionally, she started to wobble.

I'd confided in Kevin and he surprised me by saying he'd been married. I realised again that I paid little attention to other people's predicaments. He told me his story. I think it was supposed to encourage or inspire. No wonder he didn't speak much.

They had similar problems. Kevin and his wife were asked to wait a year to become pregnant naturally, but she couldn't wait and they lied after six months. As the test for a man was quick, simple and accurate, he gave a sample. He reckoned there was only one porno magazine in the room to get him in the mood.

It was entitled *Shaven*. For him, this was a big no-no. It made him think of underage girls. He liked Spanish women, he said. The hairier the better. Spanish beauty Penelope Cruz was his current favourite. He hid the porno and, despite trying to concentrate on Ms Cruz, couldn't maintain wood.

Apparently, his wife, who came from Morocco originally, was less than supportive as he explained the issue to the doctor, and they had a big argument. They had to make another appointment and left. Kevin said they went home and he gave her such a seeing-to that she was pregnant by her next period. I had no idea what the moral of the story was. Except perhaps not to go on holiday with Kevin to anywhere south of the Alps for fear of him losing control. I dared not ask why they got divorced.

Initially, I was saved from the 'giving a specimen' experience on the same day Frank came home. It was the back end of the year and a pregnancy-free Christmas loomed like a rain cloud at a wedding. He knocked, which was unusual.

'Vinnie, can I come in?'

'Sure, Frank.'

The plastic bag he passed to me had 'HMP Pentonville' on it. In fact, his tracksuit top and bottoms shouted prison on their own. He looked tired to the bone. He had to be helped to a chair, where he fell asleep within seconds. I made a cup of tea and busied myself. I was tinkering in the garage when he surfaced.

'Sorry about missing the wedding.'

'Were you in prison?'

'Not then. Just the police station. That bitch had me arrested for domestic violence. All I'd done was walk out on her and gone for some fresh air.'

'Couldn't you have come after you got out?'

'They wouldn't let me go until they knew what the situation was. In case I returned to our house and killed her. She actually came in the following day and said it was all a misunderstanding, you know, relationships. Like an idiot, I went back.'

'Go on.'

'It happened once more after a drunken row and still I went back. It was like I'd lost control of my own free will. In the end, she became completely mad and unreasonable. Accused me of cheating on her with the neighbours. All of them are retired too. So, I left.'

He stared at me then. I think to make the point he was telling the truth.

'I only got as far as the pub. She must have known where I'd go. The police arrived just as I finished my second pint. She somehow made a load of marks on her face and told them I'd hit her. The charge was assault by beating. I spent two weeks in a hellhole of a jail I hope you don't get to know.'

'When did you get out?'

'This morning. I went guilty and was given community service and a fine. The bitch never even showed up. They were okay with me coming here. You're the only family I've got. Can I stay?'

What could I say? If you told that tale to strangers in the street, they would be suspicious. If Frank's history was revealed, they would string him up from a strong branch on the nearest suitable tree.

'Of course.'

As he gave me an awkward hug, Clara came bursting through the door. She faltered and her face said 'what's he doing here?' Luckily, I could have been caught having a gang bang with The Muppets, elbow deep in Miss Piggy, and it wouldn't have mattered.

'I'm pregnant.'

She said it slow, then burst into tears, before sobbing with laughter. Frank and I weren't entirely sure what to do. I picked her off her knees and squeezed her.

'Well done, baby. Well done.'

'I'm going to ring my mum.'

She left us bemused. Frank turned to me.

'Can I still stay?'

That amused me.

'You always have a place here, Frank.'

'Great. Looks like you got plenty of food.'

That mean throwaway comment didn't pierce my mind but it should have at least made me look at Clara properly. Did I have a cold heart if my main hopes weren't so much about being a parent but rather just wishing our lives could go back to normal?

21

1996 – AGE: 30

The miscarriage happened an hour after I left for work, a month down the line. Clara had just got back from the shops and noticed blood in her pants. She flew to the hospital where they confirmed to her that the foetus had stopped developing at seven weeks. She told me afterwards it was the worst moment in her life. It wouldn't be, but she didn't know that then.

They walked her past the other pregnant mums, some of them heavily so, and left her on her own for an hour in a small room. She was given options to get rid of what remained. Let nature run its course, surgical removal or take pills and pass it at home. She chose the latter and came back a changed woman.

Our relationship became like a house on the seafront. We were taking a battering and the storm was doing its worst, but we repaired and maintained. I hoped we would be okay. The news was a terrible blow to her. I loved Clara and knew that I could survive us not having children. I wasn't sure she could.

I remember coming home that night and finding Frank ashen-faced, waiting at the gate. I still don't know why Clara didn't ring me at work and get me to go with her, or, at the least, come home. Instead, I found her in bed, fully clothed and curled up with her knees tucked in. I perched on the bed next to her. If there were words for those occasions, I'd never known them. I stroked her hair away from her face, and her blurred eyes refocused.

'Why, Vinnie? Why us?'

'I don't know, baby.'

She was like a child too, sobs shuddering her body. I got in beside her, shuffled into the spoons position and kissed her shoulders. Eventually, she settled. I slid out from behind her and went to leave the room.

'Vinnie.'

'Yes.'

'They told me I can still get pregnant. We just have to wait for a bit.'

'That's great news, we'll do it.'

As she closed her eyes again, I shut the door. The overriding emotion I felt wasn't sadness. It was anger. All the scum in the world shelling out children without a thought to the process, and a good woman like Clara had to go through this. They weren't in my house to face my wrath though. Frank would have left if he'd known what was coming down the stairs. Instead, he was making a cup of tea.

'Still here, Frank?'

I whispered the words, so as not to disturb Clara. He did the same.

'Yes, anything I can do? You want a brew?'

'I meant, why are you still here?'

He paused, mid-stir, shocked.

'I'm sorry. I didn't realise I had outstayed my welcome.'

The hurt on his face released some of my steam, but not all of it.

'Good things happen to me, don't they? When you're about. Look at all the shit you've got me in. You're a criminal. And a jinx. You pick a fight with my best man and then don't show when you've scared him off. You're great news.'

'I had your back, Vinnie. I've always had your back.'

'I don't think I could do much worse on my own. Do you? I lost a good friend because of you.'

Frank wasn't one to hold his tongue. I watched him try and fail. He hissed the words at me.

'Scott was not a good friend. He was a prick at school and he's still one now. Do you want to know why we fought? Be careful, Vinnie, you might not like the answer.'

'Spit it out. It's not as though today could get any worse.'

Then, however, it did.

'I overheard one of his mates say, "What are you hanging round with him for? He's a loser," and Scott replied, "I know, but he's got the inside with the office birds from work." His mate said, "You're the best man, aren't you?" and he said, "Yeah, I didn't want to do it though." So, I told him not to bother, and he hit me. Then you arrived.'

I would be thirty in June. Yet that quick sentence had me back at school. The person I thought I had become didn't exist. I was Vincent Roach, nothing more. I backed away from Frank, not wanting him to see how exposed I felt. His face implored me to stay.

'I'm sorry, but he was no good. He didn't deserve to be your best man. You don't know how devastated I was that I couldn't be there. I'll make it up to you, Vinnie. I promise. Remember these words. I will make it up to you.'

'Mum would have been so upset.'

'Don't judge your life by Mum's standards. She wasn't the person you think she was.'

I had no idea where he was going with that comment and staggered from the house, like Frankenstein's monster in a B-movie. I found myself in a shop and stood at the counter, staring towards the vodka. Even then, I didn't fancy it. I'd smoked on the odd occasion and so now bought a pack of twenty Berkeley, my mum's old friends, and a lighter. Finding a bench, I inhaled deeply and felt myself relax.

It wasn't Frank's fault, and it certainly wasn't Clara's. Bad things happened to me.

22

1997 – AGE: 31

Needless to say, Frank stayed. It helped. He saw a succession of women, all of whom were normal. He got a job with an engineering firm in Spalding and seemed calm and content. Clara retreated into herself for three months. It would have been like living on my own, without Frank. I didn't know the doctor had told her to wait that long before trying again. Then, the sex started. As before, I enjoyed it at the beginning after her being so distant. However, with each failed pregnancy test, it became more functional.

After a further six months, we returned to the surgery. As there had been a previous pregnancy, they examined both of us to see if we had any issues. I hoped I was the problem as any more pressure on Clara would have been unwelcome. It was a warm afternoon when we sat down in the consulting room for the doctor's conclusions. The heat in there was stifling and I removed my coat. Although I think I was just looking to do anything to eat up a few more seconds of waiting.

The lady came in with a smile and opened a window. I could

hear birds and cars in the distance. The air smelt of summer. It didn't feel like a day for bad news.

'How are you both?'

We smiled, too nervous to make a sound.

'Right, well, the news is mostly positive.'

We breathed out in unison.

'The results from the X-ray showed that one of your fallopian tubes is blocked. Therefore, the egg can't reach the uterus and the sperm can't reach the egg. The good news is that your other tube is functioning as it should and you will be able to get pregnant in the normal way. Vincent, your motility and count are excellent. Any questions?'

Our silence continued as we tried to process the massive amount of information that she had condensed into a short paragraph. Clara broke first and challenged her sunny demeanour.

'Does that mean it will take twice as long to get pregnant, and can't you unblock the other tube?'

'The tube is blocked in such a way that surgery is unlikely to be successful. We don't think it's necessary as we hope you'll fall within two years.'

'Two years?' I was sitting next to Clara and still got sprayed with spit. The consultant must have been drenched.

'Yes. There are IVF options further down the line, but there are no physical reasons inside why you shouldn't get pregnant. We can give you fertility drugs to increase the chances of ovulating on the side with the open tube. However, the ovary on the blocked tube side can migrate across to the tube that isn't blocked, so hopefully it would be quicker. I should point out you are significantly overweight, Clara. Twenty-one stone is morbidly obese. It's unlikely IVF would be approved without substantial weight loss. Every pound you lose now will assist you in getting pregnant naturally. If that fails, we could try IVF and you would already be more likely to get accepted.'

Jesus Christ, I thought. Twenty-one stone. I knew glancing at her would be a bad idea, but unfortunately, I couldn't help myself. My head swivelled round, up and down, and then back again. She looked at me out of the corner of her eye. Her clothes disguised her size, that much was obvious. No wonder she'd been leaving them on lately when we were intimate. It wasn't news to her though as she didn't even blush. Another thought came.

'Doctor, why is the tube blocked? Couldn't the same happen to the other one?'

The doctor's cheeks bloomed.

'Well, there are many reasons for that sort of thing.'

'What are they?'

As she reeled them off, I turned to look at Clara again.

'Endometriosis, appendix surgery, previous ectopic pregnancy, a uterine infection caused by an abortion or miscarriage, or the most common cause of blocked fallopian tubes is pelvic inflammatory disease from a prior or current STD.'

Clara flinched at the end of the symptoms. Involuntarily and guiltily. I'd never had an STD and Clara was a virgin when she met me. Or so she said. I didn't need to ask the doctor what she thought the cause might be as the earlier symptoms had been ruled out.

We were both quiet again as we drove home. It was only as we neared our road that Clara spoke.

'I'll lose the weight, Vinnie. I'll get us a baby.'

Other thoughts were swirling in my mind. Ones about lying virgins. I decided, there and then, not to look backwards. We had gone too far to dredge up the past. Clara's happiness was my focus. Besides, now we both had blood on our hands.

Some new neighbours were moving in next door to us as we

pulled up outside our house. I was about to say we should introduce ourselves to them when I saw a woman come out of their front door. I think 'about to drop' is the phrase most often used. I didn't need to look at Clara this time to see her reaction. I got out of the car and helped her inside. Then, I was scared.

23

1999 – AGE: 33

Clara was true to her word, and the pounds dropped off. We got healthy together and I can say that, for perhaps the last time, we were happy. I thought the neighbours' twins being born would be a constant reminder of our own predicament, but it spurred Clara on. When she hit fifteen stone, she miscarried a baby at eight weeks. Further tests revealed that she had only one functioning ovary, luckily on the side with the unblocked tube.

I feared this news would cause her to fold, but she proved to be made of stronger stuff than I imagined. I could tell she was blaming herself, somehow thinking it was because she was too heavy we lost that child. However, her single-mindedness was inspiring.

She got down to twelve stone near Christmas and then two lines appeared on the pregnancy tester again. The festive period was a flurry of fond memories. We put our old clothes on and giggled at how they hung. I kept mine due to my usual lack of confidence. Clara threw hers out, saying she would never be that big again.

Even Frank got pulled into the celebrations. He wasn't a big

Christmas fan, but he laughed along at the Uncle Frank jokes. I'd not thought what his views were on the child thing. It was his family too.

Their relationship was strained still. If I left them in a room together for any length of time, one of them would make an excuse to leave. I presumed he wouldn't stay when the baby came. I was no expert, but sleeping with a crying infant wasn't high on anyone's living requirements.

He would be missed though. He had calmed down. He had a good job, a nice girl and a flash car. We didn't see much of him as he went to the gym every day. Maybe that was what settled him down. The poor girlfriend was keen, but Frank had no interest in having his own children.

The doctor arranged an early appointment at the hospital for us due to the problems we'd had. It was the day before the scan when Frank told us he was leaving. He'd bought a place in the town centre a year or so back and rented it out. The tenant had left and he would now go there himself.

'It's time for me to leave.'

'That's okay. It's been nice having you here.'

'I won't be far, so you can ring me any time you like. I'll even get one of those mobile phones so you can get hold of me at work.'

'Fingers crossed that won't be necessary.'

'No, it won't. You've done well. You have a family. A beautiful wife, a good job and a baby on the way. If any of my girlfriends looked at me how Clara looks at you, I'd run for the hills. Mum would be proud. She always told me to watch out for you, Vinnie. I know I've not been a great brother, but look at you. You've made it.'

'When will you leave?'

'I'll pack this afternoon and tonight, and leave tomorrow. You know I travel light so it won't take too long. I might even hoover before I go.'

'You are a changed man. Mum would've liked that too.'

He went to climb the stairs and stopped. Taking a moment to decide, he returned and altered my perception of the past.

'Vinnie, I have to tell you this. I don't even know why, but for some reason it's eating me up inside and I need to get it out.'

'What is it?'

A crazy thought flashed through my mind. Was Clara's child his? Was that why they seemed so uncomfortable together?

'I know you have Mum on a pedestal, but she wasn't perfect. Far from it, in fact. Mum killed Dad.'

'What? His heart failed.'

'Yes, but she caused it. She smothered him with a pillow. He had no quality of life and was suffering. She said it was for the best.'

To be honest, I wasn't surprised.

'When did she tell you? Before she died?'

'No, before she did it. She asked me to take you away to Cromer, remember. She didn't want either of us here when, well, you know.'

I wondered if life had made me hard. All the death and disappointment seemed to have blunted my feelings. I'd never been a strong one for emotion. Frank was almost crying.

'I'm sorry. It was selfish to burden you.'

'That's okay, Frank. It will be our secret. She did what had to be done. That's all.'

Clara woke up and screamed in the middle of the night. I pulled the bed covers away expecting to see blood, but there wasn't any. She was in agony though. I carried her to the Fiesta, quite a task, and laid her on the back seat. The drive took forever. It's slow time when your dreams are dying.

I parked in an ambulance bay and lifted her up. As I passed through the sliding doors, her howls of pain worked better than any bell. They placed her on a trolley and demanded I move my car. She's pregnant, I told them.

It took no time at all for me to park up and return. By then, she had been taken to a room and staff surrounded her. I suppose some can blame the NHS for many things, yet it can't be denied, they are fantastic in a crisis. She was bleeding and her stomach was strangely distended, as if she were nine months gone, not nine weeks. An ectopic pregnancy was suspected.

What happened afterwards was a blur. It was as if it were all over in minutes. However, I was there for hours and hours. Later, they let me wait in the high dependency unit as all three beds were empty and then they wheeled her in. The nurse wouldn't tell me anything, except she would make a full recovery. Basically, she lied.

She looked small, grey and frail in the bed as if she were dead. Blood loss, I learned. I held her hand and stared at her. I had no idea how long for. She had no make-up on, but I realised I'd forgotten how pretty she was. She who spent so little on herself. The doctor came and explained. Their prognosis was correct. It was all rather technical to a man like me, but the final solution had been a radical hysterectomy. They almost lost her at one point. Even I knew what that meant.

I stayed that night, as did a nurse. Clara did come around, but refused to talk to either of us. I left as the hospital woke up and drove home. The neighbour waved as I pulled up. She was pushing her children in a double buggy. I sat on the concrete ramp at the back of the house where Mum smoked, and I did the same. Was that what life did to her?

My brother's comments gave me some clarity over the past. I remembered her as a serious woman. The hugs had seemed stilted and uncomfortable. We'd had to rebuild our relationship after my accident. It had been strange to sleep in a house with people I didn't know. To be touched and kissed by strangers. Had it been easier for them, knowing they loved me but wondering what remained? Or easier for me, starting from scratch?

Maybe that was why I had begun to think I might like having my own children. So I could experience through them the missing years of my own life. At that point, I understood I would never get to be a better or worse parent than my own. My mum used to say your children's judgement was all that matters. I wouldn't be having any, so who would judge me?

My brother disturbed me, carrying a box. I vaguely remembered seeing his car outside but it hadn't registered.

'This is the last few bits.'

'We lost the baby, Frank. And any chance of another.'

I expected him to give me platitudes; instead his reply was simple.

'I'm sorry, but maybe that's for the best.'

As he walked past me, there wasn't even a curl of anger at his cold remark. There was a part of me that knew it was true.

It wasn't just the baby that died. I suppose it wasn't a baby at that stage, more a collection of cells, but bereavement was what we would feel, for that life, and also for our hopes and desires. Something deep inside Clara's mind disappeared that day and our future went with it.

24

My brother inspired me to get a buy-to-let property. We suddenly had a large amount of money put aside with no purpose. I suppose I could have bought a new car but I enjoyed the challenge of keeping the old Fiesta on the road. Silent Kevin carried on coming over to work on it with me. Still brought us two beers each.

The money saved to pay for cots and clothes would never be used for that purpose. Clara didn't go back to her job after that, so our income dropped, but she wasn't spending any money in bed. In a perverse way, she had her maternity leave.

I couldn't say I blamed her. Myself? I simply stopped thinking about it, or perhaps I would have folded too. There were constant reminders when you went out, young children on television programmes at home, and they even knocked on your door, once in a while, at Halloween. The little sods were everywhere. They aren't something you notice if you are young. I suppose it's like when you're single, all you can see are couples holding hands.

The doctor came to the house. I couldn't get Clara to go to the surgery. He offered all manner of things to help. Medicines, therapy, counselling, and even acupuncture. She took none of them. I believe she would have killed herself if she didn't have an inbuilt enjoyment of food.

It's a sign of human nature that there is usually something we like to do that's both a reason for living and is detrimental to our well-being. I think my mum's was smoking. The perils of that were obvious, yet she gained a great deal of relaxation and pleasure from it. I loved to read, but it cut me off from society. My brother drank alcohol. He could put up with five days of the heaviest graft during the week if he had eight pints of lager waiting for him on a Friday night. Clara liked to eat.

I wouldn't have thought it was possible to get to twenty-one stone if you didn't. It was a shame after the hard work. All that effort to lose the weight and none at all to put it back on.

I'd seen those television shows on feeders and that was what I became. A reluctant one, at least, as I never stopped trying to get her involved in life. That was the truth while I lived there anyway, but later I gave up. Nonetheless, it was still me who went to the shops. I was also the waiter who brought a nice strong tray to make my job easier.

It was only when eating that she seemed to wake up from the stupor. We would have conversations around food. To start with, it was just to ask what she wanted. Later, I decided to make meals at home and she would be interested. Sometimes she came downstairs and we cooked together.

We had some good laughs; I was a terrible chef at the beginning. I still don't understand how two people can follow a recipe and get a completely different result. However, I had my Clara back and, even though she refused to go outside, that was enough.

I carried on working at Perkins, reading, and bowling. It didn't feel like much of a life. Clara watched a lot of movies. That was an improvement on before, where she just studied the wall. Bit by bit, she almost returned to normal.

We had a cold spell and she used the telephone to order double glazing. I thought that was a big deal and she was getting better, until the day they came. I took the morning off at her request and all I could hear as the windows were replaced were the shrieks of play from next door.

The idea of buying somewhere else lit her up though. We browsed the *Evening Telegraph* property section each Thursday and she even got into the car to see the place we found.

It was a first-floor flat in Paston, not far from us. I wanted it close so I could keep an eye on things. It was in a terrible condition. The previous tenants had been drug addicts, and the owner just wanted to get rid. I found we could afford to buy it outright.

I wondered if Clara would be put off by the mess but she saw the potential. It was spacious: big bedrooms, a huge lounge and loads of storage. Clara could look past the stench and debris, and knew it would make a nice home for someone. We put it in her name for tax purposes.

It was my brother who suggested we move to the new place and rent out our old house. Clara jumped at the chance. Real enthusiasm was enough to defeat any doubts I felt about moving into a flat, and I would not miss the garden, which was becoming a ball ache.

Frank and Silent Kevin came and helped on removal day. Clara wouldn't let us touch her wardrobe and she carried a jewellery box with her as if it held the Crown jewels. The only jewellery I knew she had of any value, she wore on her fingers all the time. I hadn't seen that particular box before either.

More strange behaviour wasn't much of a surprise so I didn't mention it. Kevin acquired a van for the big stuff. We binned loads of it. Clara wanted fresh things for our new start.

It was weird walking through the bare rooms afterwards. I kept getting flashbacks: my dad watching the snooker with drool coming out of his mouth; my mum smoking whilst doing the washing; a younger version of me doing weights, sitting on the edge of the bed.

A blurred image came to me, of feeling silent rage in a small dark space. I checked the cupboard under the stairs. The white paint on the door was peeling so badly the wood was visible. Did I get stuck in there once?

It was empty now, and the slim key lost long ago. Frank must have cleared it. It made me think of the loft. We'd never been allowed up there; in fact, the hatch was still secured with a heavy lock.

We found a bunch of keys at the back of one of the drawers. I grabbed the stepladders and went to see. There was only one that looked like it would fit and, sure enough, it did. I pushed and twisted the wooden cover and lowered it down, bringing a waft of dust and stale air. How long had my mum been dead? Thirteen years. In some ways, my life hadn't moved on. I was glad we were leaving now.

As I climbed the steps a feeling of dread came over me. Why hadn't I been up here before? But who went in the loft unless you'd run out of space downstairs? I began to think that something terrible was up there. Something best left forgotten. I was right, but not in the way I suspected. There were no bodies. They were elsewhere.

The space was empty save for a rusting pram, a kid's bicycle, and a couple of cardboard boxes. I carried the two boxes down, sat on the bottom step of the stairs and opened the first one. It was full of children's toys. They looked old and loved. Well, perhaps unloved as many of them had been decapitated.

None of them looked familiar to me except one. An Action

Man. The torso, one leg and the figure's dirty jacket; Frank's favourite toy. I could see him doing swoops with him as though he were flying. My mum wasn't a nostalgic person, so it was nice to think of her putting these away to show us in the future.

The second box had paperwork in. I was about to close it back up when I saw an official letter. It was from Her Majesty's Prison Service. In the name of my mother. I scanned through the pages like a speed reader, my eyes widening as I searched for answers. I was so engrossed that I didn't hear my brother come in and stand next to me. It took a while, but I saw what I was looking for.

'Grievous Bodily Harm,' I said out loud.

'Four years at HMP Holloway,' he replied.

I searched his face.

'You knew?'

'Yes.'

'She told you?'

'No, I found out. A long time ago. I was going to tell you, but I know you looked up to Mum so much that I took the easy way out and kept it to myself.'

'Perhaps you'd better tell me now.'

He seemed relieved. Another burden he would be free of.

'When I was released from the navy I travelled all over and visited where Mum grew up. I had some beers in a pub and mentioned it to some old guy at the bar. Turns out Mum was famous. After a lot of asking around, I found someone who knew her. He told me what happened.'

'Do I want to hear this?'

'I think you should. It's important to understand where we came from. Mum met Dad at the local dance hall. He was smitten and she was determined. He was engaged though. The details are vague.

'The story he liked was that Mum went looking for her, with a knife, and picked a fight. She almost killed the girl and was lucky not to be tried for attempted murder. Her solicitor muddied the water, saying it was the other girl's weapon, how she started it, and our mum was only protecting herself.

'The judge and the jury believed Mum's version of things, or at least there was enough doubt. The problem was she stabbed her over twenty times. Mostly in the extremities so she would suffer. Four years was possibly on the light side.'

'Bloody hell. That was unexpected.'

Frank gave me an odd look.

'You're all emotion, Vinnie. Anyway, Dad waited for her. Everyone disowned them both, they moved away and never went back. We had grandparents, aunts, uncles, cousins. Many of them dead now. For want of a better phrase, Mum was a fruitcake. She had a terrible temper. She killed our cat, for fuck's sake.'

'Spike? Wasn't he run over?'

'Mum did him with a meat tenderiser for stealing a steak she left on the side. Then put the body at the side of the road so we'd think he was hit by a car. It was flat enough.'

'How do you know that?'

'I came in and found her wiping blood off the walls. There was fur on the floor and a bloody mallet.'

'What kind of lunatic kills a cat?'

'A psychotic one, like our mum. Mum knew she was deranged and she also understood that I was aware. We used to row, but never in front of you. That was the reason our relationship was so strained. Oddly, it was you coming along that calmed her down. Even so, you must have seen her blistering temper?'

'I don't really remember. She was always so nice to me.'

'She was worried about you. That's why. We all were. There's other stuff I probably should tell you too, but that's enough for one day.'

'Why would Dad stay with someone like that?'

'Love, I guess. Remember how you were when you came back from that holiday with Sara? You were a different person. Someone who others wanted to be with. As we know too well, life is short. If you found someone who made you feel like that, why would you let it go? I've never had it. I suspect most people don't.

'The person we look for, whether we think it or not, is one who brings us alive. Otherwise, we're just existing. Even if you only had it for a few days, you understand. That's not a dig at Clara. Life isn't easy and it's also hard to explain or analyse.'

I looked at Frank after he spoke those words and wondered who he was. I still thought of him as the fighting boy at school. He'd be forty before he knew it. It was too late for Sara and me.

Yet, I remembered. How many years since would I trade for a few more hours with her? Who was I for those few days and what had I now become? Should I accept my current situation or was I doing us both a disservice? Maybe things were happening as they were because us being together wasn't meant to be.

I thought of my mother and her stoicism. Family, she'd ingrained in me, was the only thing. You married for life. Accepted what came. There was no escape and why would you want one? Those beliefs were written through me like an image through seaside rock. I never thought Clara would be the one to give up.

25

2000 – AGE: 34

There were four flats in the block where we lived. The two on the ground floor were occupied by single mothers. One was well-spoken and aloof. She had a Down's syndrome boy called Jonty. He seemed such a lovely chap, so happy. Yet, he was wary around me. Sometimes he would run off when I spoke to him, so in the end I left him alone.

The lady underneath, Michelle, was a nightmare. In the first month we were there I saw at least five different blokes leaving early in the morning. She must have made a poor cup of coffee as they seemed in a rush to go.

Michelle had a daughter called Kirsty who always appeared at a loose end. She looked seven years old, yet seemed to be left to wander the streets after school. There was another lad a bit older than her who played with her and Jonty, and I would often hear the three of them giggling together.

For some reason, children laughing didn't bother Clara so much there. Perhaps it was because they were past the baby and toddler stage. It made me wistful though. There was a round-about at the back of the flats, and I would find myself staring at them through the lounge window. It must be nice to have your own son. Someone to show the world to.

Clara had seen enough of the world and only left the house to go with me to the supermarket. I couldn't remember when she'd stopped driving. Perhaps about the time I no longer went to the bowling alley. It was almost as if our horizons were narrowing together.

One Sunday springs to mind. As I pulled up outside the flats, Clara and I saw that Jonty kid point at me and run away. I remembered feeling hurt and thinking maybe I could bring him round with comics or sweets. I knew I must ask his mum first or they would suspect I was some kind of pervert.

The car sagged with a week's shopping when Clara got out as I'd used it to counterbalance her weight.

'Can you manage that box, love? I'll carry the bags.'

She picked it up with a grimace. It only had twenty-four cans of Coke in it, yet she carried it in as if it were a seven-stone bowling ball. I followed her up the stairs. She had to stop and rest every few steps. There was no way I could have got past her anyway. She took up the whole width and had to carry the drinks in front of her.

The lad from next door hovered behind us. I heard him say, 'Typical,' under his breath. When had she become so big? We finally got inside, and she dropped on the floor like I imagine an Ironman might after a tight finish.

'You okay?'

She refused to answer, or maybe the way she hauled breath into her lungs meant she couldn't. I wasn't to know at the time, but she wouldn't leave the flat for nine years. Years tick by. Lives are wasted. I suspect if Clara knew what was to happen, she would've left that day and never come back.

26

2001 – AGE: 35

As time dragged by, the neighbours accepted me. I enjoyed watching the children grow up. The boy next door, Ben, was a bit lively, but he had a good heart. Kirsty, in the flat below, was our favourite.

Michelle, her mother, came up one Saturday night and said an emergency had occurred. Would we look after Kirsty for her later until she got back? She would only be an hour or so. I was surprised that she bothered to ask. Locking her up in her own home alone seemed safer than what she often did, which was to leave her outside and pay no attention. Of course, we said yes.

Kirsty always looked bewildered to me. Like she felt she didn't belong anywhere. Her mother was a raging pisshead. She would have got on well with Frank. Neglect was probably the wrong word. Kirsty just had an unloved air about her. It must have been a strange thing, not living with your father. It was a terrible shock to us when we lost our dad and we were much older than eight.

The cheeky mare knocked on our door after teatime, ushered her daughter in and said see you in an hour. I hoped she'd kissed Kirsty goodbye and explained things before she brought her round, as she left in a rush without doing either. I pondered what kind of emergency would call for high heels and that amount of lipstick. Kirsty and I regarded each other in a cloud of perfume. She edged into the lounge when asked.

She sat in the middle of the sofa and stared at Clara with a suspicious air. As though she had come over for dinner and was wondering if she was the starter. I hadn't thought about what Clara must look like by that point. Our scales went no further than twenty-four stone.

When Clara mounted them a few months back, I saw the pointer hit the maximum and bend as it yearned to go further. I was behind her at the time, a fact she was unaware of until I gasped. Again, neither of us said a word and nothing changed.

She had a two-seater sofa, which she overwhelmed as I would a child's armchair. Clara offered Kirsty a chocolate from the ever-present Quality Street tin she kept on a small table beside her. Kirsty went over, took one, popped it in her mouth, and made a hmmm sound. She looked at Clara, side to side, and with a grin said, 'You must have eaten a lot of these.'

She spoke so factually that we both roared with laughter. All fact and no tact, as May used to say. I turned the channel to *Bugs Bunny*. She looked over, smiled and came and sat next to me on the three-seater sofa. We watched hours of cartoons that night.

It was lovely to watch Kirsty giggle at the interactions on kids' telly. After a few episodes, she began to relax and point things out to us.

'The rabbit's behind that tree. He doesn't know.'

Clara and I kept stealing glances and smiles at each other. I think I saw her cry once, but she had been laughing hard a few seconds before so it was difficult to tell. It wasn't a time for sad thoughts. More a case of being sent a glimpse of happiness and trying to enjoy and store up every moment.

This was the sort of thing she had planned for our lives. Simple pleasures and innocent times. We had pie and chips around eight o'clock. It was gone nine when I first gave a thought to where Kirsty's mother was.

We didn't have a contact number or even a hint of where she'd gone. Kirsty didn't seem to care, and we'd been sent a small piece of sunshine, so I wasn't too worried. At nine-thirty, though, I wondered what time was normal for a kid of her age to go to sleep.

'When does your mum take you to bed?'

She looked at me in a strange way.

'I usually put myself to bed as Mum's already asleep on the sofa.'

If sentences can hide long sad tales, then that was one.

'My friend at school gets a bedtime story when her mum or dad put her to bed.'

Clara and I exchanged another glance. It was heartbreaking but not our business. I didn't even know if one of the many men who had visited downstairs was her dad. Asking her would be a downer if one of them wasn't. My indecision was solved by the doorbell buzzing repeatedly.

I opened the door to Michelle. She didn't explain, or apologise for taking so long. Perhaps the beer was going off at the local pub and they needed volunteers to stop it being wasted. Maybe she was the only one who turned up.

'Come on, you,' she slurred at Kirsty.

'Ah, Mum. Do I have to?'

Michelle seemed to consider it for a second but was beyond any rational thought so just spun around and left. No words of goodbye or thanks. She never told me what the emergency was. I doubt she could remember anyway.

It was about this time that I started to have a recurring dream.

I'd wake up in a sweat, shaking with fear. By that point I was sleeping alone. There wasn't enough room in the marital bed for both of us.

The dream, nightmare really, was always the same. A small boy clung to the top of a slide, wanting to get off. Another kid was halfway up and banging the space between them with a small sturdy branch while another watched on. For some reason, the children wore masks – a sheep, a wolf and a shepherd. I could see the sheep crying. The wolf didn't care, enjoyed it and banged harder. I heard the shepherd shout, 'Leave him alone, let him down.'

After what seemed like an eternity in my dream, the sheep lost control of his bladder and urine poured down the slide, causing the wolf to slip to the bottom. The wolf sloped off, satisfied, and the shepherd comforted the victim.

27

2002 – AGE: 36

Clara tried to lose weight. The broken scales might have been a motivator; however, it was when her foot went through the base of the shower that she realised things were out of hand. I bought much healthier food, we cut back on the takeaways, and she lost a few pounds. She complained that the weight wouldn't come off.

Her mum had been a help the previous time she dieted, but it made me realise I hadn't seen her parents since we'd moved in. It had been years too. They'd never been for tea at the old house either, although Clara and her mother used to meet up for dinner or shopping in the town centre. Clearly that hadn't happened with her agoraphobia. Still, I would not judge her familial issues when mine had to be worse.

The problem was her inactivity meant she burned little energy.

'It won't come off, Vincent. I need a tummy tuck thing.'

I couldn't stop myself rolling my eyes. She was somewhat off needing one of those.

'I think you are supposed to lose the weight first, and then have cosmetic surgery.'

'What's that other thing they do to dieters?'

'A gastric bypass?'

'Oh yeah. Where you can only eat small meals.'

'That's right. We could probably get that for free on the NHS.'

I could see her mind ticking at the thought of going to the doctor and all the rigmarole. I wondered whether she thought, if we paid for it, they would come and do it at the flat.

'We could buy a treadmill?'

'Really, Vinnie. Could you see me on one of them?'

That tickled both of us and we laughed.

'How about we get it and I put my mouth one end and you can keep sending cakes down. Does that count as your ten minutes of exercise?'

'I expect so. If I alternated with grapes and strawberries, perhaps the odd melon, you could get your five a day too.'

'Best I keep my eyes open, or you'll be slipping a banana on there.'

It seemed a long while since the two of us had chatted and flirted like that. We ended up going to bed and having sex. She was so big that it didn't work in the missionary position, so we did it doggy style. It was unusual, to be honest. I felt a bit like one of those small Indian blokes, riding his elephant.

I'm a bloke though, so I still enjoyed it. If I'd known it would be the last moment we would be together in that way, I'd have probably taken more time.

Other than my brother, one of Clara's friends, and Silent Kevin on two occasions, no-one else had been in the flat except us. Frank was the only person who had been round that year. I could tell by the look on his face that he wasn't impressed with our lifestyle. To his credit, he never mentioned it.

I understood the reason behind our actions, or lack of them. We hid from the world. A life wasted is a terrible thing. While others died and suffered, we withered, of our own free will. Clara knew that too, yet seemed powerless to change.

We were trying to gain control by not exposing ourselves to new experiences. We didn't take any risks, except with our health. No more bowling, nights out or weekends away. Just an endless procession of monotonous takeaways, which we spooned into our mouths like unthinking robots. If life scares you, avoid it. I cowered in my books and Clara shrank in front of the television.

Sometimes I found myself thinking of travelling. It was as though I had someone else's memories. I imagined deserted white beaches with a warm Caribbean breeze, or being on a high mountain top with an icy Himalayan blast on my face.

I was always alone. I wondered if those thoughts meant anything. Perhaps I just watched too many travel programmes. Why wasn't Clara there? Should I reach for those possibilities or accept them as part of a life I would never know? Those things signified freedom to me. Instead, I had an existence in a jail of my own making.

Despite our risk-averse lifestyle I still felt anxious. If I let my mind roam, it would search for dark places. I imagined losing my job, dreadful neighbours moving in, or maybe I would develop an awful illness. Neither of us were criminals, yet we committed a terrible crime. One of ignoring our lives. We were given the gift of life, yet it sat between us unopened.

28

Oddly, it was Michelle, the woman living underneath us, getting a permanent boyfriend that was the catalyst for the horror that unfolded. She couldn't have picked a more unsuitable beau if she'd tried. He had an irritating nickname for one – Titch. You can imagine, he was far from small. He was the type of person who loved to talk about himself, mostly of him winning at various things.

Clara had begun to get out of breath just moving around the flat, so I took my cigarettes downstairs out the front of the flats. Although Michelle smoked like a cooling tower in her lounge, he often came outside. I think he used to wait for me to come out, just so he had someone to impress. I had few pleasures in life, so him ruining one was a constant source of irritation.

Titch was full of shit. We've all known people like him. They start off telling you a story which may be true, or, at least, have an element of truth in it. Then when you aren't amazed, they embellish it. I used to just not listen. However, if you say nothing, they create some enormous fantasy which is so clearly untrue it's a complete insult to your intelligence.

His dad took him fishing once. Fair enough, probably happened. By the end of the tale he had won a competition he hadn't even entered, and been asked to represent the county. If I hadn't peppered the conversation with a few 'Wow!'s and 'No way!' I bet he would have told me Moby Dick was nestled in his bathtub.

I used to smoke fast, so I didn't have to listen to his constant moaning about the state of the flat. When I enquired why he didn't clean it himself, he looked in the distance with a face like someone who had bitten down on a soft biscuit. That was his other quality: he had a temper. He scared me, and Michelle, I think, but he also frightened her daughter, Kirsty. That was unacceptable in my book. Still, it was because of him that we got to spend more time with her.

What triggered it was an incident with Frank. Titch had a habit of talking to you and poking you in the chest with his finger to get his point across. It was bizarre. When he was doing it, I couldn't believe I would just stand there whilst this total invasion of my personal space was happening. In fact, it was hard enough to be classified as assault. What could I do? He must have been two metres tall. Frank pulled up and misread the situation.

'Get your hands off him.'

Titch's chin dropped, and he regarded my brother in the same way a lion might do if a gazelle had come over and browsed his CD collection. I'd never seen Frank look as scared as he did that day. Age mellows most of us and he was a different man, so you had to admire his courage.

He wasn't daft though, and pushed me through the door and up the stairs. Titch's face still had the 'does not compute' expression on it when we left. It looked like I would smoke out of the kitchen window in future. Clara rarely got off the sofa nowadays and complained the smell blew back in, but I would rather upset her than spend any more time with the meathead below.

'What was all that about?' Frank remained flustered when we reached my flat.

'He's Michelle's boyfriend. He wasn't actually doing anything, he's just a bit aggressive.'

'It's Titch Ryhall, the boxer. You knew that?'

'No, I don't follow boxing.'

'He was in the news for biting someone's ear off in The Windmill pub on Lincoln Road.'

'That does ring a bell. He mentions fighting all the time – I assumed he meant in pubs. Didn't he go to prison for that?'

'Yes, he's only been out a few months. He's barred from most places in town for starting fights, although he left jail with a reputation as someone reasonable.'

That didn't make any sense.

'I don't get it.'

'He spent eighteen months at Her Majesty's Pleasure and, with his celebrity boxing status, he got a job at the prison gym. State of the art, I'm told. His drug of choice was ecstasy, preferably with gallons of Stella. A cell is not the sort of place where you would want to combine those two substances, even if you were able to get your hands on them. They were the things that ruined his career. All of a sudden, he's clean and training again. When he leaves, he's fit and toned, but, along with many ex-cons, he can't control himself on the out.'

'So, when he gets out, the supply chain is reopened, and he returns to his old leisure pursuits. He's a fit, hard, professional boxer abusing class A drugs and alcohol.'

'Yep, and, Vinnie, he knocked out our darts captain because he looked at him weird.'

'Did he?'

'What?'

'Look at him funny?'

Frank looked at me funny.

'I think you're missing the point, Vinnie. If you must know, he said all he did was raise an eyebrow at him. He woke up in hospital and only remembered buying his first drink.'

'Fantastic. And you've just wound him up downstairs.'

'I was protecting you, Vinnie.'

'Haven't you learnt? All you're doing is getting me in more trouble. The fight in Cromer, all the shit at school, even my stag do. Don't bother again.'

'You don't understand.'

'Don't I? Frank, trouble follows you. It always has, ever since you were young. You got chucked out the navy. Then you killed that bloke in your car.'

'Killed what bloke?'

'In that accident you had.'

'I wasn't driving, he was. It was black ice. An accident.'

'What about that boy from school who died?'

His face flared with anger, but worry was present too. He went to leave and I grabbed his coat.

'Tell me you weren't involved with that.'

He mumbled something that sounded like 'wusma'.

'What was that?'

He turned around and bellowed at me.

'It was Mum!'

'Don't talk shite,' sprang from my mouth at the same time as an old memory surfaced. Just after the news of the tragedy came out, she asked me if school was better now. I didn't think too much of it. It was a weird thing to say, but she had been drinking. I remembered her expression. Like she had done something and wanted a reward.

'You're right. I was involved. Just not how you're thinking. That boy was picking on you at school. He was too big for me to do much about it and had loads of mates, so he laughed when I told him to stop with the bullying. He said you started it anyway.

'I told Mum. She knew who he was. His whole family were renowned for their shitty behaviour. I never thought for a million years she would do what she did. She said it was an opportune crime. He'd bunked off school and was jumping off the footpath bridge at Ferry Meadows. The one people used to swim underneath. As he was about to jump, Mum hit him on the head with a hammer. The coroner thought he misjudged his landing, struck the stones in the shallows and drowned.'

'What was she doing there with a hammer?'

'Exactly. Premeditated, not opportune.'

'She told you all this?'

'More or less. Just before she took care of Dad, she confirmed it.'

'You've carried all this knowledge with you, all these years, without telling anyone?'

'Yep. I think it's what caused me to go off the rails. Should I have told someone?'

'Yes, me!'

'She had me swear that I wouldn't tell you. I didn't mean to now. I just don't want you thinking I'm like her.'

'Fucking hell, killing a child.'

I could believe it though.

'Let's hope her madness isn't hereditary. You can imagine what phrase rolled out of her mouth afterwards.'

It didn't need to be said. I could hear her saying it. She only did what had to be done.

29

2003 – AGE: 37

After that first babysit request with Kirsty, she stayed at ours on the odd occasion. Mostly Saturday nights for a few hours. We wouldn't have minded if Michelle had said she wanted to go for a few drinks, but she always used the phrase 'something's come up'. We called them EAAs. Emergency Alcohol Appointments. We looked forward to them.

Kirsty was at that charming stage just before she got to senior school and noticed boys, celebrities and face paint. She loved Chinese food, so she fitted in great. It became a treat for all of us when she was left at ours.

New Year's Eve was the first time Michelle didn't come home until the morning. I woke up on the sofa with Kirsty nestled in beside me. Clara must have put a blanket over us and gone to bed. It was 9 a.m. when Michelle banged on our door and staggered in. She looked absolutely off her face.

Alcohol doesn't change people like that. She could only have been on one or a range of recreational substances. She made no sense. Apologising with one breath and then accusing us of stealing her child with another. She virtually pulled her sleeping daughter onto the floor and dragged her down the steps. Kirsty's howls tore at my heart as they went out of sight. What could we do though? I was only her neighbour.

Kids are resilient and non-judgemental. They don't seem to remember things the way we do. Kirsty said afterwards her mum was sorry and just tired. Then she carried on as normal. Whereas those cries stayed with me for a long time. Michelle had been tired a lot since she met Titch.

The upside was that she was hardly functioning. She and Titch were almost dissolving before our eyes. He became furtive, shifty and hostile, in stark contrast to how he was before when he was aggressive and confrontational. More a caged rat than a cage fighter.

We began to have Kirsty all weekend and the odd day in the week. I would sleep in the lounge and she would have my bed. It was the closest we would come to having a child of our own.

Frank avoided us after the Titch incident. I can't blame him for his fear. To my surprise, Titch never mentioned it when I next saw him. No doubt so wasted, he struggled to remember whether he'd dreamt it. Michelle would appear with the odd bruised arm or other marks on her face that her heavy make-up couldn't hide. Her clothes hung on her and she would only be seen after dusk.

I hoped Titch wasn't hurting Kirsty. One night, she stayed over and seemed listless and was uninterested in her food. She spoke little and went to bed early. I hovered outside her room and could hear her cry.

A few days later, I came back from work and found someone's feet sticking out of the gas meter cupboard next to the entrance to the flats. They were huge dirty trainers. I leaned in and there was Titch, face buried in the rubbish that always collected in there.

The smell was terrible. It reminded me of my dad just before my mum killed him. It was a bitterly cold night and the street was empty. I returned to my car and took a heavy wrench from my toolbox.

All I could think about was Kirsty crying in our flat. I could feel the anger rising in me. In all likelihood, Titch was responsible. That poor excuse for a living creature would be missed and mourned by no one. I checked to make sure nobody had ventured out, then pulled him into the enclosed space, closing the door behind me. There was room for me to stand above him.

Unless animals had been doing their business in there, and poorly ones at that, he had soiled himself. That, combined with his heavy nasal snoring, did not endear him to me enough for any leniency. What were the chances of me getting away with this act? My breath smoked out in front of me as I raised my hand. A bright light seemed to go off in my brain – I paused. Instead of accomplishing the killing blow, I thought of Clara.

She had problems with bedsores. Her GP noticed as soon as he arrived. I suppose he was looking out for their unwelcome arrival, like flies to a corpse. Clara complained to him of burning or itching. He showed me how to rub the Cavillon cream in and that became part of our day.

Who would do that for her if I was gone? The spell was broken, and I remembered I didn't know if Titch had definitely been violent to them. It was likely, but I wasn't in a position to take action at that moment.

In light of Frank's revelations concerning our mother, I'd logged on to the work computer and researched her conviction. I hoped they didn't check anyone's browsing history. I deleted it, but who knows what they can do nowadays? It was clear my mum had issues, and I worried what I might uncover.

I found one item about it. It was an interview, with a picture of a younger version of the lady who had sat at the back of my mum's funeral. The article mentioned the death of her daughter from cancer and how she blamed that 'psycho' for ruining her life all those years ago and how her daughter hadn't recovered.

It mentioned my mum being diagnosed as having borderline personality disorder. I didn't know what that meant, but, on reading more, it fitted. She was more reckless and ruthless, not cold and calculating. My mum had been in prison at least once, and was an impulsive creature. Violent, remorseless, with a blatant disregard for the rights of others.

However, she was nervous and easily agitated and certainly not a criminal genius. She had a genuine love for her family too, which I suspect a psychopath would never have had. All these thoughts went through my mind and the wrench became heavy. I was none of those things, so I lowered the weapon.

I rolled him onto his front and adjusted his clothing. He was freezing to the touch. We would let God decide. I wandered back to the car and replaced the tool, then, whistling under my breath, returned to my wife.

30

2004 – AGE: 38

Much to everyone's surprise, Titch's untimely demise from hypothermia hit Michelle hard. For someone who led such a violent life it was a let-off for him to die so peacefully. I thought she would be relieved to escape his heavy embrace.

Instead, her chaotic existence continued, as did her legendary consumption of alcohol. The couple who lived across the landing appeared to be losing their battle too. They suffered in silence, so things carried on as they were and nothing was said.

Kirsty was quieter the older she got. She only blossomed when she was round ours. It was the only place where she could be a child. I often saw her battling with shopping bags from the supermarket or hanging washing on the line. Ten was no age to be taking on that kind of responsibility.

We invited her over whenever possible. Sometimes she came, other times I caught her taking rubbish out, the chink of the empty bottles betraying their presence. Or I'd peek through her window and see her hoovering. Michelle would be unconscious on the floor and oblivious.

Clara's health was suffering too. The doctor warned her that she was doing permanent damage and must make changes to her lifestyle. Some days she didn't get out of bed. I was distracted by Kirsty, who was often teary. Her life was a struggle that her inexperienced self couldn't cope with.

Most nights she curled up on the sofa next to me after having a shower at ours. She often did because hers was broken. I wasn't sure what that meant entirely, but she wouldn't let me round to help tidy, never mind see her bathroom so I could fix it. Kirsty was a good girl, still protecting her mum.

Like most kids, she never wanted to go to bed.

'It's not fair.'

'Come on. It's late now.'

'No, not that, life.'

'What isn't fair about life?'

'Why some people have a dad and others don't.'

'I know, poppet. Life can be tough. My dad died when I was fairly young.'

'At least you knew him. There's something wrong with my mum too. She sleeps and cries. I don't understand. I thought we'd be happy now that horrible man has gone.'

'So did I. You will be, I'm sure of it. Up you get, I'll tuck you in.'

'Can't we just sleep on here? I'm warm and cosy.'

'You'll sleep better in bed. You can properly relax.'

'He wanted me to call him Daddy.'

Long seconds stretched out as I considered her words. I stared in at a minefield.

'Really?'

'Yes, but I didn't. You are more my dad than he was.'

'Well, thank you for saying that.'

'Will you read me a story?'

'What do you fancy? *Gruffalo*, *Lady and the Tramp*, or *Beauty and the Beast*?'

They were her favourites.

'*Lady and the Tramp* or *The Gruffalo*. The Beast is dead.'

Out of the mouths of babes.

'Come on, then. Quiet now, so we don't wake Clara.'

We sneaked past Clara's door and gave each other a conspiratorial smile. Both books were read in the end, and she seemed to quieten down.

'It's chilly in here. Will you get in for a bit and keep me warm? Like that picture there.'

It was the part of the book she loved. Where the Lady and the Tramp pose with their puppies next to the Christmas tree. A happy family. Still, I wasn't sure where the boundaries were, in a relationship like ours. It was cold in that room though; the heater had long given up.

'Okay, shift over. Only for a while, mind.'

She snuggled into me and I felt a tear sting my cheek. Yes, people had it all, they just didn't know it. Michelle was neglecting what some would trade anything they owned to possess. Again, it felt to me that good folk suffered.

I pushed her hair behind her ears and marvelled at her skin; so soft and blemish free. Her pyjamas smelt of flowers too, from the washing powder I'd used.

'I'm safe here, Vincent. You aren't going anywhere, are you? You'll look after me, won't you?'

'I won't leave. Shush now and sleep.'

I loved that about children. Their ability to go to sleep in seconds. As her breathing settled and delicate snores crept out, my own eyelids felt heavy. I thought of the words she'd spoken.

'Of course, I'll protect you, child,' I whispered into her hair. 'I already have.'

My eyes closed. I caught a glimpse in my mind of the jacket that I removed from Titch that freezing night, in case God needed a helping hand to make the right choice.

31

2005 – AGE: 39

The time that I look back on when it really went wrong was the day that I saved Clara's life. It was a hot August Saturday. One of those days the British say they wish it were like every day, and then moan about. Her breathing that afternoon was rasping and heavy. One of her legs seemed to have swollen up too. I should have known she was struggling as she failed to finish her dinner that night. She retired to bed early and left us watching TV.

As I was eased from a deep sleep, I thought Darth Vader was in the room. I lay there and listened to the slow, restricted sucking in of air.

'What are you doing, Vinnie?' She gasped.

Her large bulk blocked much of the light from the hallway, although there was enough for me to decipher disgust on her face.

'I said, what are you doing?'

She gurgled the last sentence out and wobbled on her stick. I knew what she meant and understood how it'd look. I stole from Kirsty's bed. When I pulled the duvet back, you could see she only had a pair of pants on.

Should I look guilty? Had I done wrong?

'Nothing. She couldn't sleep. She said she was scared.'

'It's 5 a.m. How long have you been in there?'

'Does it matter? She was crying, Clara. You know how messed up she is.'

'It's not right, Vinnie. You know it's not right.'

Her breathing reminded me of my dad's death rattle. She collapsed to her knees with a sob and I saw the pale blue her face had become. Clara whispered with her final remaining piece of air.

'Ambulance, can't breathe.'

After muttering those last words, she fell to the floor and ended up wedged on all fours in the doorway. Like an enormous grizzly bear, sleeping where it fancied.

I had to stand on the small of her back to leave the room. With a lot of sweating, and advice from the emergency operator, I dragged her into the recovery position. Her breathing settled to match that of Kirsty, who still slept. I held her hand as we waited for them to arrive. I felt her squeeze mine and found her eyes glaring. She wasted no words. I listened as each line stung.

'I'm to blame too.'

'I knew where you were.'

'I should've stopped you before.'

'How long's it been going on?'

Her grip on my hand crushed. Her glare demanded an answer.

'I've done nothing wrong,' I said.

'Oh, Vinnie.'

'I was just comforting her.'

'That's what my father said.'

32

2006 – AGE: 40

Clara didn't leave hospital for months. She was in a terrible state. Her blood pressure was at a level that was bursting vessels in her eyes, and they were concerned with the condition of her heart. That, combined with type two diabetes, underactive thyroid, kidney problems, and her total inability to do any exercise meant they were loath to let her go until she stabilised.

With encouragement, she lost weight and increased her mobility. They gave me a day when she was allowed home.

Clara never mentioned what had happened. I supposed most marriages had secrets; however ours was quite a burden. All she said was that Kirsty wasn't allowed over any more. We had carried on the same while Clara remained in hospital. When I let that slip, Clara was furious.

Kirsty said she preferred it when it was just the two of us. I was dreading telling her, but the day Clara came home I had no choice.

'Clara comes back today.'

'That's a shame.'

'I don't know how to say this, Kirsty. She doesn't want you coming around any more.'

'What? Until when?'

'Ever, I think.'

I'd always thought Kirsty was beautiful, but rage could distort even a child's face into something dreadful.

'Bitch. She's jealous because you love spending time with me. Tell her to piss off.'

'I can't do that, she's my wife. Watch your language too, Kirsty. I've told you about that.'

Rage turned to anger, focused on me.

'So, you're leaving me too, are you? Like everyone else does. Worse. You're sending me away. Am I that disgusting?'

I didn't want to tell her the truth, but I couldn't concoct a slant where she might not think it was her fault.

'Clara says it's unhealthy us spending time together. I'm not your father, I'm just a neighbour. So, you shouldn't sleep here.'

Kirsty wasn't listening though. She walked to the door, turned back and spat on the floor. I'd seen her mother do that. The vision of hatred was chilling.

It took six months of maintaining a slow rate of weight loss and an increase in exercise before they would consider something more dramatic to get her to a healthy size. Clara was brave. She'd insisted on walking to the ambulance when it arrived that fateful morning. I'm not sure how we'd have got her down otherwise, and she insisted on walking back up when we returned. Then she rose at 5 a.m. most mornings, I assumed so she didn't meet anyone, and strode round the neighbourhood.

We didn't talk much during that period. We slept in separate beds still and only came together to eat and watch TV. Grievances faded, and the ice thawed as, yet again, food brought us closer. She didn't waver through that time. As for me, all I could think was at that rate of loss she would be sixty before she finished. The specialist agreed. He explained what he recommended.

'Cutting back on food triggers biological systems that evolved when humans needed to survive in times of scarcity. Once people have become overweight, their biology changes. Their bodies want them to return to the maximum weight they achieved. They have complicated biological signals that tell their body they should be thirty stone still. Few individuals completely recover from obesity; rather they suffer from "obesity in remission". It's temporary.'

Discouraging news.

'In your case, you've made good progress and we're now happy to go ahead with surgery. This isn't a quick fix. If it's successful, I don't see any reason why you shouldn't be able to get back to around twelve stone. This extreme and rapid weight loss will hopefully change your biological make-up and it might be possible to return to eating normally.

'There are risks. People have died, although that is rare. Psychologically, the hardest part can be at the end of the process as you will be left with excess skin. That should be removed at some point. It's unlikely the NHS will pay for that though. I would expect this whole process to take a minimum of two years.'

As we walked out into the sunlight, I prayed for strength and luck. I didn't believe in God, yet someone was listening.

33

2007 – AGE: 41

It did take Clara the best part of two years to lose a significant amount of weight. A gastric bypass is far from a magic wand. I lost weight in sympathy, but wasn't committed either. I'd done bad things in my life and forgot them. So it was strange that I was wracked with guilt over my sneaky Big Mac habit. While poor Clara was ticking off the minutes until her next crispbread, I would pretend I had to go to work early or stay late. Then, like a desperate junkie in a badly lit car park, I took my fix.

I must have smelt of fast food but Clara didn't mention it. I found the odd chocolate bar and ice cream wrapper in the bottom of our bin or even, once, hidden inside a book. She said some things still went down easily. I said nothing. She couldn't have been cheating too much as just before Christmas the doctor informed her that she had lost ten stone.

It seemed crazy that, after all this time, she was only halfway there. The worst part was that she didn't appear much different. You could have argued that she looked worse as the skin now drooped around her and it looked like she was melting. She would still sit in her chair in the same clothes anyway.

She needed to keep going and then, when she stabilised, skin-removal surgery came next. However, they wouldn't pay for it. Fifteen thousand pounds was a serious amount of money, but if that was what Clara wanted, that was what she would get. I'd have to take a loan out to cover it. However, we were dealt an ace, and I didn't need to.

Clara always liked to watch the National Lottery show on a Saturday night. I hated it. The chances of you winning were negligible, so you were virtually guaranteed a depressing start to your evening.

We'd just been informed that our neighbour had died of cancer. It only registered then that I hadn't seen much of him. Should we have done more? We were hardly close. Nevertheless, we were subdued. That day I'd already endured some mind-numbing shows. The balance of power had shifted in our relationship. I dared not upset her as I didn't know what she would say.

'Come on, Vinnie. You check those.'

I'd thought my life was pathetic before that moment. It felt as though it couldn't get any lower. I would be wrong on so many levels, but that night was different.

The first number came out, and I didn't have it on any of my lines. The familiar sinking feeling began. I gave a half-hearted cheer for the second number and a whoop when I matched the third. Silence for the following two, then simply, 'Shit,' as the last number came up. A few seconds later, I matched the bonus number.

'I matched five.'

'Check them again.'

I did. I couldn't believe it. 'We won, we bloody well won!'

'Shhh,' she said.

Clara got up and took the ticket off me. She looked at the

screen and gave a small smile. As if life owed her that much. There were no cheers or high-fives. No hugs, or shouts of where shall we go. She flicked over to a Christmas quiz and I picked up my book, safe in the knowledge our marriage was over. The ticket wasn't returned.

I didn't think matching five numbers would pay a fortune, a few grand perhaps, so it was the following afternoon when I checked. A hundred grand, as it turned out. I don't know how Michelle downstairs found out, but she was aware. When I told Clara how much it was, she knew too.

It's funny how life can be like that. We didn't need the money and yet we got it. Desperate others went without. I understood luck. It was a volatile lover, and mine was about to run out.

34

2008 – AGE: 42

Clara booked her first operation for May. She needn't have done so as our world fell apart before that. I was allowed to buy a Porsche. That may seem extravagant, however it was possible to pick up a nice second hand one for ten thousand pounds.

The car, crazily, changed my enjoyment of life. At least for a while. I felt cocooned in its plush interior. I got a small buzz whenever another Porsche driver would give me a nod or a wave. Inside that car, I was a different man. A fast man with places to be.

I cleaned and valeted it with purpose. I tinkered with every free moment. Silent Kevin came over and shared my passion. I would never leave Clara. That's not what marriage is all about.

However, as we bonded again over the car, I realised Kevin and me could go to rallies. Or even go on a driving holiday. How cool would that be? Maybe around Scotland, all the scenery, hills and deserted roads would make for a fantastic time. It's strange, but I could have done all these things before. I'm sure Clara wouldn't have objected. You often see clearly when it's too late.

Clara lost focus and put three stone back on. I hadn't noticed but the lad next door and his mate had stolen some cigarettes. Ben and Jake knew I smoked and came to my door. The price was too good to be true, so I agreed.

When I went to get my wallet from the lounge, for some reason the little shitbags followed me. I'm not sure who was most surprised, us or them. I suspect they'd never seen Clara. Maybe they thought she didn't exist, or that I'd killed her. Anyway, the look of amazement on their faces when they entered the room renewed her efforts.

That same afternoon, one of the little toads threw a golf ball through our first-floor window. It was closed at the time. It landed in a bowl of soup I was eating, splashing the boiling-hot contents on my groin. I leapt out of my seat, spilling more of the scalding product on my thighs. I had to pull my trousers and pants off to stop the burning sensation.

When I got to the window, I saw them both running away. Clara watched me for a few seconds. Then burst out laughing. It was a sign of our marriage that, as the tears rolled down her face, I couldn't remember the last time she'd laughed like that. Despite the window, I considered joining in, but my nuts were stinging.

Those young lads had spoken about ten words to me before we had that win. Not all of them had been complimentary. Now I had a sports car they waited for me when I came home from work. I would often take them out for a drive, one at a time. I felt like a celebrity. It was a good feeling.

It made me pine for the children I knew I would never have. There would be no son to share life's experiences. I saw little of Kirsty or her mother. Both would avoid me if they could, and I them.

The police turned up in mid-May, just before I left for work. I was staring out of the window as my car looked like it had dirt on it. I kept it pristine and idly wondered if I had time to take it to the wash. My loyalty card owed me a free one.

I allowed myself a smile as I assumed the boys in blue were there for the scallywag next door. I was surprised it had taken so long to put an end to his thieving ways. Two vans and a squad car seemed excessive for one urchin. It was a shock when our door rattled in its frame. Then, even though I had done nothing wrong, I realised I somehow expected them.

I opened the door and in they swept. A badge blurred my vision. They ushered me into the lounge where a plain-clothed man read me my rights. Rape of a child under thirteen. I was stunned to silence. There was a lot of aggression in that room. I could hear them looking in the rest of the flat. They cuffed me where I stood, staring at Clara. Her face was impassive. It was only as they forced me out of the room that I called out to her.

'Clara, tell them. I didn't do anything wrong. Please.'

Nothing from her and a growled, 'Move,' from an officer.

They weren't gentle as they shoved me down the stairs. Michelle's door was open. She bobbed there with a hard, determined look on her ravaged face. I couldn't see Kirsty, and for that I was grateful. My shoulders hurt as I reached the last step and leant back to stretch them.

The officers saw that as resistance and my head was lowered further. They bounced me through the main door and out into the light. My first sight as my vision cleared was my beautiful car. It wasn't perfect any more, far from it. In fact, there didn't appear to be a single piece of it that wasn't damaged, cracked or pierced.

There were more uniforms and gawping passers-by as I strained to see. The next image was the face of my neighbour's son, Ben, whom I had thought they had come for, as he came back from the bins. Our eyes met and nothing. That hurt more than the car. We'd lived next door to each other for almost a decade, and I didn't matter enough for him to be bothered.

In the police car, I was in shock. My brain was so startled by what I heard that it shut down. There must have been a mistake. Kirsty, the neighbour's daughter from downstairs, had accused me of abusing her. For years. The contempt and scorn on every single face as I was taken into the police station was vivid. I imagine if they'd wheeled an enormous rotting pumpkin in, their expressions would have been the same.

When they described the charges, I tried to explain. No one believed me. I told them I did occasionally get in bed with her but just so I could offer some comfort and warmth. The girl was vulnerable, I said. Yes, she had been coming over for years and of course I cared for her.

Did we cuddle under the blanket on the sofa? Yes, we did. It was all innocent. I didn't do any of those terrible things. There were pages and pages of incidents with dates. Almost as if someone had been keeping a diary.

Each time that I nodded to confirm that I had indeed taken her for a walk in the woods, or bought her sweets, they grimaced and scribbled in their books. I said I didn't need a solicitor as I was innocent. It was a terrible mistake.

The scornful looks in their eyes flashed between disdain and incredulity. They were rough with me as I was forced back to the cells. I realised the severity of it all and called for a solicitor. When he turned up, he was about as respectful as the man who brought me my phlegm-filled sandwich.

Hours later, they allowed me a phone call. I have no idea how long afterwards that was, but night was falling. I should have rung Frank because Clara didn't pick up. There were no second chances and again I was frog-marched back to my blue mat. It felt like I was in the bowels of the building. Time had no meaning in that place. I would find the true horror in that statement over the coming months.

The following morning, I appeared at the magistrates' court. All I did was confirm my name, and the judge ordered me to silence when I tried to speak. It was too serious a case for them. I was remanded in custody and taken to the basement of the court-house. The solicitor finally came to see me. At least his professionalism had returned.

'Do you understand what happened there, Mr Roach?'

'No, can I go home now?'

'Sadly not. You've been charged with extremely worrying crimes. Some of which carry a life sentence.'

'I haven't killed anyone?'

'Rape of a child under thirteen. Repeated occurrences over many years. Cold and calculated. You admitted to being there on all the occasions too. What were you thinking?'

'I was there, but we only cuddled.'

'If you don't understand what's wrong with that statement, with a neighbour's child, then you will be sent to prison for a long, long time.'

'What? I'm just going to get taken to jail, right now? What happened to innocent until proven guilty?'

'It's not a case of that because there's a minor involved. You live in the same block of flats. Her safety is paramount. The police will want to know where you are. You can apply for a bail hearing through your new solicitor. They'll look to offer you bail if you have somewhere to go. As long as they don't think you are a danger to that poor young girl.'

'New solicitor?'

'Yes, this is beyond my experience.'

He looked relieved as he continued.

'You need a specialist solicitor and a knowledgeable barrister.

Preferably both of them would have successfully defended paedophiles. I warn you, they are expensive.'

'This isn't right, I'm innocent.'

'Vincent, they have a signed statement, saying you got into the bed of an unrelated ten-year-old girl. Whether you cuddled her *or* had sex with her is neither here nor there. You will go to prison. It's just a matter of how long for.'

35

They dragged me from the cramped darkness of the prison van and I understood my predicament. Barbed wire, stark walls and unforgiving faces greeted me. As I was processed, stripped and searched, I began to think straight. The hostility of the police and courts had gone. Here, I was just a number. I thought they must have seen every kind of person through there.

When they put me in a room to wait to see the nurse, I mentioned that hopefully I shouldn't be there long. A look of complete disinterest closed my mouth. I was on a production line. Speed and efficiency made them happy, so I kept my silence.

A large bald officer sat me down and took my photo. A minute later, I had an ID card. I waited to be bundled to the next area. Instead, he smiled.

'That's some serious charges.'

'I know. I'm innocent though.'

'All sex offenders are.'

I considered that piece of information while he got some paperwork together. I could see how this was going to go.

'No one cares, then?'

'About what?'

'Whether I did it.'

'Here, no. Everyone lies here. Me included.' He tried to make a joke, but it wasn't funny. 'Perhaps the truth's too horrible to admit.'

Guilty, until proven guilty. Prison all the way.

'So, best just get on with it? Do your time, don't complain too much, because nobody gives a shit?'

That didn't sound fair.

'That's it. You got it. Now, you've come with nothing, so you will receive a prison tracksuit and pumps to wear if you want. You'll get personal items on the wing: towel, toothbrush, soap etc. You have induction tomorrow, where they will explain everything. In the meantime, keep your head down.'

'What about getting bail and a solicitor?'

'They'll explain tomorrow.'

'That's it?'

'You'll need to sign this compact for the Safeguarding Wing.'

'What's a compact?'

'It's an agreement that you will abide by the rules on the Safeguarding Wing.'

'What's a Safeguarding Wing?'

'It's where they put prisoners like you.'

'Like me?'

'Yes, people who have been charged with sex offences.'

'So, I go to a wing with rapists, perverts and kiddy-fiddlers, even though I may not actually be one.'

He looked confused for a second.

'Why can't I just be on the normal wings? They won't know what I'm in for, unless I tell them.'

Then he looked amused.

'Mr Roach, I don't have time to be kind to your feelings. I say it how it is. I've been here long enough to have learnt that's the best way. If I put you on normal location, they will ask you where your paperwork is and when they see you are in for offences against minors, you will be assaulted. Seriously.'

'What if I don't tell them?'

'It's not *Mastermind* here, so you won't be allowed to pass on the question. Unfortunately, you look a bit like a sex offender with that quiff. You also don't appear very threatening. Fair game for any bully. I suspect you may get your head kicked in even if you were only in for fraud.'

I signed the paperwork.

'You can make one phone call here too. I'll need to dial the number and introduce the call. Just to ensure that they want to speak to you.'

I was about to complain when I realised they thought I might contact my victim. I knew this call was important for my immediate well-being. I didn't waste it this time, and Frank picked up on the first ring.

'Frank, it's Vincent.'

'Heh, how's thing's, Vinnie? Long time no hear. Your phone been broken?'

'Not exactly. I'm in prison, Frank. It's serious. I need a solicitor. A good one. You're my only phone call, so I need to know you'll help. Can you go to my house and make sure Clara is all right? She will explain. I don't understand how it works here, Frank. I'm scared.'

I could almost hear Frank's brain clicking through the facts.

'No problem. I'll sort it out. Try not to worry and of course I'll look after Clara for you.'

'Frank, I think I have to go. Apparently, I will be able to ring again tomorrow from the wing. Please pick up.'

'I won't let you down, Vinnie. You can always rely on me.'

As the line went dead I realised I hadn't even told him why I was there. He also hadn't asked. In fact, he didn't sound surprised.

* * *

The officer explained that it was 'after bang-up' as we walked to the wing. I assumed that meant everyone would be in their cells. I hadn't been looking forward to arriving to a busy wing in chaos, and my pulse eased. He passed my file to an officer with a lined face who peered at me like he was checking the small print on a contract.

'Stick him in twenty-three.'

When we got to the door, the man produced a bunch of heavy keys and slid a stiff bolt across. He stared through a panel before he unlocked it and gestured for me to enter. There was a sour smell in the room and I could hear guttural snoring as I walked in. I stopped and reversed out.

'I was told I would be in a single cell.'

The officer's almost amused expression changed.

'Who told you that?'

'The man at Reception.'

'He lied. Get in.'

I felt something light up in the dark recesses of my brain. I'd had enough bullshit for one day.

'No. He said I needed to be "risk assessed" first. As I might be a killer.'

He looked through me for a few seconds, before shouting out, 'Birchall!'

The officer with the craggy looks came over.

'He says he wants a single.'

'Really? You go home, son. I'll deal with this.'

The other officer left at a canter. I supposed even the staff didn't want to stay there any longer than necessary.

'Why do you want a single?'

'I was told I'd be "risk assessed". I need to get my thoughts together too. I'll do that best on my own.'

'Okay. I'm assessing you now. Your file says you have been accused of interfering with a child. Therefore, your risk is extremely high. To children. Your cellmate is an old man. So, there's no danger here.'

I needed an outlet for my anger. He was all that was available. He must have seen the change on my face because he spoke as I took a deep breath.

'Mr Roach, to be honest we don't have any single cells left tonight. You will be going in here whether you walk in, or we drag you in. Think about it, a guy like you, first time in prison, you need a buddy here. The guy in here's a doctor. Was, a doctor. He knows the ropes. Talk to him, let him explain what you should and shouldn't do. Don't make any silly mistakes. He will know about your chances at court, too. He's been here more times than I have.'

What was I thinking? Anger or violence weren't my friends. I stepped inside again and was pleased that the grunting had settled to a mild grumble. Maybe that was how it would be for me. Small wins were all I could hope for.

As the door closed, I realised I hadn't been given a toothbrush and my teeth felt like they had been prepared for painting.

'Hey, I was supposed to get a toiletry pack when I got here.'

The man peeked round and smiled.

'Out of stock, I'm afraid.'

36

I didn't sleep. The lack of a pillow was a hindrance to that, but my mind was churning. I had chosen phone credit over a tobacco pack on arrival. When the door shut, I regretted that decision. The cell smelt of smoke though and there was a pack of Amber Leaf tobacco, a box of filter tips, and rolling paper on the small tabletop. I stared at it for a while. I even reached out for it once and pulled my hand back.

The man on the bottom bunk farted at that moment. Our eyes met.

'First night?'

'Yes.'

I was judged for a second time that day.

'Smoke as much as you like, I got plenty.'

He then rolled over and immediately began snoring again. I took his advice. I almost didn't want the night to end. I felt safe with cigarettes and memories. However, the future beckoned. What kind of existence would I wake up to? How could my life change just like that in such a short space of time?

The solicitor's words at the courthouse weakened my heart every time my brain recalled them. 'It's just a matter of how long for.' I remembered the film *The Shawshank Redemption*. All the guys in the yard joking that their lawyer had fucked them. It seemed I had fucked myself.

My mum had instilled in us many things. Some were awful; an ability to be sent to prison included, but she'd given us a sense of stoicism. That was a gift. By the time the jail stirred to life, I had accepted my situation. I needed a bloody good barrister, Frank's help and some luck. I would only get one of them.

Doc, as my cellmate insisted on being called, was an interesting man. He looked and appeared exactly like what he was – a GP. Even down to the wispy hair and half-moon glasses. 'Was' being the operative word. His offending had put an end to his practising many decades ago.

His alarm went off at six-thirty and he got up, shaved, pissed and dressed while whistling. He said nothing in all that time. My stress levels began to rise. I could handle the silence no longer.

'Thanks for the tobacco.'

'No problem, I practically heard you looking at it.'

'It really helped, so I appreciate it.'

'I'm Albert Gilroy, but most people call me Doc.' He paused and gave me a thoughtful look. 'Weird how I was stopped from working, but when I came to prison I resumed business, so to speak.'

'You diagnose problems?'

'To a degree. Mostly I tell folk not to worry. There's too much time for that here.'

'And you're guilty?'

'Yes, I suppose I am. Sick, I would call it. I love to touch young boys. Not sexually, just examine them. Weird, eh?'

Sick was being generous, I thought. The officer at Reception had been honest with me, so I decided to go for the same route.

'But if you were getting off on examining them, then it was sexual, wasn't it?'

'Well, the juries agreed with you, so I was sent to prison. That was forty years ago, the first time anyway. I've been in and out ever since. I only spoke to a boy at the paper shop this occasion and got sent back. They gave me a whole year here, just for saying hello.'

I was expecting fear in that unfamiliar place, so being freaked out was welcome. The door opened at that point, a voice shouted, 'Breakfast!' and the sound of human movement echoed into the cell.

'No one wants to leave their cell when they first arrive.' This amused him. 'Come to the door. It's not so bad on this wing.'

I followed him there with a racing panic and looked out at the creatures shambling towards an open servery. It resembled a scene from the film *Cocoon*, before they bathed in the special pool. A long line of geriatrics in tracksuits queuing at a hatch. However, instead of old women, we had strange young men. They wore haircuts that didn't match their faces, and had eyes that liked the floor.

A muscular man with a short Mohican walked down the stairs with just a towel wrapped round his waist. He strolled to the front of the queue and slammed his bowl down whilst staring around looking for non-existent challenges.

'That's Kilkenny. A bully. Don't worry, he won't bother you while you're with me.'

That was a good thing, as he looked unpleasant to say the least.

'Why is he on here if he's like that?'

'He's still a sex offender. He raped a woman. What he actually did was break into a house whilst high on cocaine and alcohol. He found a lady in her bed, removed her feeding tube and raped her. Your average Joe doesn't like that sort of thing, so we have the pleasure of his company on this wing. Here, he is a big fish as, due to the nature of the beasts, most offenders are dirty old men or sick young ones.'

We watched as he walked up to an emaciated person who might have been any age from twenty to seventy. He took the carton of milk out of his hand and climbed back up the stairs. His victim shrugged; it was clearly not a new experience. He came over to us and spoke to Doc.

'Can I borrow a milk later?'

'Go on, take one from my stash.'

When what I could just about recognise as a young lad moved past us into the cell, my curiosity got the better of me.

'Has he got cancer or something?'

'Who, Karen? No. Heroin addiction. Drugs like that suppress your appetite and lead to malnutrition due to long periods without eating. Karen's resources are so depleted, his body is now consuming muscle tissue and facial fat, giving him that gaunt hollowed-out appearance.'

I imagined Karen's response if Clara had placed our normal Chinese order in front of him. His eyeballs would blow out.

'I take it he didn't fancy his chances with Kilkenny.'

'No one does. Kilkenny's a twenty-three-year-old weight-lifting machine. In this place, he is King.'

'Why doesn't he bother you?'

'I helped him when he first arrived, like I will help you. Wait here, I'll get you a bowl and your breakfast.'

Was it possible to help a man like me?

When the lad came back out of our cell, clutching two cartons of milk, I smiled at him. He shrugged at the fact he had taken two.

The drugs must have consumed his conscience as well as his future.

'Doc's a nice guy,' I said.

'Not if you're a young boy.'

I gave him a look of confusion.

'Aren't you a young boy?'

He leered a toothless grin. 'Not young enough for Doc.'

The answer to whether Doc was able to help me was yes and no. The only person who came through for me outside the prison was Frank. He organised the legal team and everything else, except Clara. She wouldn't open the door to him. Just told him to go away. The flat and the savings account, where the lottery winnings resided, were in her name. All I had was my parents' house, which, after evicting the tenants, I had to sell at auction to raise the funds for my defence. It was 2008 – not a good time to sell.

During that time, I couldn't bring myself to believe Kirsty would stand up in court and say I'd done those things. As the months ticked by and I read the evidence against me, I saw it was her word against mine. I'd already admitted to half of it. What jury would believe I had got in bed with her and just cuddled? Even me going in her room and hugging her was going to sound like a horrific crime if told in the wrong context.

My brother offered me a room at his place if I was given bail, but it was too close to the flat. There were bail hostels, but again they were too near to Kirsty, unless I wanted to move to Nottingham. From what Doc told me of such places, they were not for the faint-hearted.

It was all academic because I was refused bail anyway. The judge was of the opinion I'd serve custodial time whatever happened, so I might as well start ticking the days off straight away. That was how he said it, like he was doing me a favour.

Doc was right about Kilkenny. He gave me the odd filthy look but left me alone. The others were not so lucky. Every Thursday when our canteen arrived, he entered most cells, like a taxman, taking his dues. Some resisted and they would be bruised and beaten shortly after.

As I said, he was smart. The officers looked for this sort of thing on canteen day, so he left it for a few days. I suspect he knew the waiting was almost worse. I'm not sure if the officers were aware the wing was being dominated by one person and ignored it, accepting that someone had to run the show, or if they generally didn't give a shit.

Most were professional in their dealings with us, but others were of the impression we were in prison for punishment. If you asked them for help, they laughed in your face.

Kilkenny was sick and extremely violent, but he wasn't stupid. He was polite and chatty with the officers. The wing was clean and tidy. No one caused any problems when it was time for bang-up. Everyone existed within his reach. He was the leader, and he made the rules as he went along. The punishments were swift and ferocious. We lived in fear. Nobody could stand up to him.

Even though I was left to my own devices, I was still humiliated. One time, as we sat cowering, I listened to him 'visit' the man in the cell next to us. There was no talking, just the sounds of someone being beaten.

That poor victim snapped that night. He swallowed toilet paper and drank water afterwards so it expanded in his throat. They found him in time but I believe he was sectioned. He had seemed relatively normal before that too, friendly even. We never saw him again. Afterwards, I asked Doc why nobody did anything, or told the officers. His reply was chilling.

'He's too strong. Most of us on here are weak-minded and weak-bodied. If we attacked him, even a load of us, and it went wrong, he would be here when we woke up the next day. Then he would visit us individually like rats in a trap. As for telling the officers? It's our word against his. This is a prison so information leaks. I don't want to think about Kilkenny's revenge if he found out he'd been grassed up. So, we sit and suffer. Don't get noticed. Better someone else than us.'

37

In hindsight, it was the uncertainty of what was going to happen that damaged me. If you have an operation approaching, you want it over with, otherwise it dominates you, and you are reduced to being the sum of that worry. Our justice system takes months, sometimes years.

When they brought me back from sentencing, six months had passed. I hadn't absorbed the magnitude of what could occur by the time I returned. Even then, I would struggle to get my head round it.

As the day approached, I took my barrister's advice and changed my plea to guilty. If I made Kirsty testify to what I had done there would only be one winner. Who would you choose? An innocent sobbing twelve-year-old or a forty-two-year-old pervert? I even shaved my hair off after thinking what that officer said about how I looked. Afterwards, I resembled a threatening nonce as opposed to a quiffed one.

If I had pleaded guilty straight away, I would have been given a third off my final sentence. That's for saving the taxpayer time and money, and for saving the victim any further suffering by having to give evidence. My late change of heart was another mistake.

'Vincent Roach, you appear a measured man. One who isn't prone to rash behaviour. This means I consider the events premeditated and pre-planned. You groomed the mother and child over many years. In all my time in the courts, I have yet to come across such sickening and deceitful actions. These kinds of organised cold acts are hard to believe.

'You are an extremely dangerous man. A person capable of such deeds is likely to commit further horrendous crimes. In my experience, these behaviours are present from a young age and I wonder what other sins you may have committed before this. Society, in particular the children, need protecting from evil men like you.

'I am compelled to give you a 10 per cent reduction in your sentence due to your late guilty plea as the law regrettably directs me. Therefore, I commit you to eighteen years. Take him down.'

The officer booking me back into the prison looked interested this time. As though I might explode or sprout wings. Strange, then, that it was such an effort to put one leg in front of the other. In fact, I wanted to lie on the floor.

I'm not sure why I stopped myself having a breakdown. I thought it might be pride, but you leave that outside those walls. The little of mine I had left was still in the courtroom. They took me to a small room.

'How are you feeling, Mr Roach?'

My jaw froze. How did I feel? I felt like a terrible error of judgement had been made. One that, any minute now, someone would turn up and rectify. That was a feeling I carried with me for many years. I would come to hear many others say almost those exact words. There are cells full of people with a common state of mind. All of them thinking that they shouldn't be there.

'Do you want to speak to anyone? A listener, maybe? Eighteen years is a long, long time. I would be terrified.'

He summed me up in that final sentence. I was petrified. I was frightened about where I was going, what would happen to me, and, worst of all, if I could survive. When others looked at me, though, they didn't see my concerns. They saw an impassive face, and a man they didn't understand. People struggle with the unknown, and it was easy to be afraid.

Humans are amazing creatures. They have an astonishing ability to adapt. Even as he droned on, my brain was trying to process the information. Eighteen years meant serving nine years. Then I became free. On licence but away from this place. I was a sex offender so would have to inform the authorities of where I was all the time. How would I survive? As always, books would be my friends.

Still, I could move. Maybe to the seaside, somewhere remote. Although the cash from my house was gone, wasted on an awful unnecessary defence. Screw them. I could live on benefits. I didn't need money. There would only be me to support.

The now irritated officer rapped his knuckles on the desk to get my attention. He had the cheek to be annoyed.

'I've got a form to fill in!'

I stretched my jaw and spat the words at him.

'Do I feel sad and depressed? Yes. Am I going to kill myself? No, I'm not. So, tick your boxes, sign your form and fuck off with your fake pity.'

Again, a strange uncontrollable burst of rage had swarmed through me, out of nowhere. I could not have prevented it, even if I'd wanted to. His face was almost respectful.

'Thank you. Sign here and you can go.'

As the violent fury left my body, I just put a cross on his form. He avoided my stare. Somehow, I knew I would end up here. It was as though I'd come home. That was always my destination, and each decision I made simply accelerated my arrival. As I stepped through the office door and looked for where to go next, his voice followed me out.

'Yo, Eighteen! You left your ID card.'

The name stuck.

They called me Eighteen, but I didn't do it.

38

2009 – AGE: 43

Frank was the only person who came to visit me all year. You would think that depressing, but I was grateful. Many on our unit had no one at all. The things they found us guilty of are hard to forgive. Whenever children are involved, sympathy is in short supply.

Suicide, self-harm and depression regularly swept through the wing like a virus. It would go quiet for a few days, then someone else would fold. This seemed to remind others of the futility of their existence and they would consider their options. Of course, fear was everywhere. Fear for the future was the real killer.

Any kind of conviction for a sex offence against children was a death sentence for your old life. There would be no going back to your family or friends. The streets of your youth wouldn't want you. Places of work, worship and play tried to forget you existed. Perhaps people whispered your name on dark days.

You were sent to prison and dropped in a sea of human failures. Then you drowned, while the ripple effect tore through those who knew you. Who recognised the signs? Why didn't anyone notice? Or, what should we have done?

You have a lot of time to think behind bars. Your worries are inescapable. Where would you go when you were released? Would you ever work again? Who would help when you came out with nothing? People shun the sick and evil; they are unloved and unwanted. A life alone is something few can endure.

As I was now sentenced, I was assigned an offender manager and a resettlement officer. An appointment was made for me at a place called 'The Link' to see them both. I had to be escorted from my wing by an officer, as the mainstream prisoners were liable to assault anyone they suspected of coming off the 'nonce wing'. The resettlement officer was first. He took me into a small booth and opened a file.

'Sit down, Mr Roach. How are you?'

'Fine, thank you.'

'Right. My job is to make sure you prepare for your release. Housing, jobs, that sort of thing. Do you have somewhere to go when you're released?'

I'd lost my house, but I hoped I wouldn't be homeless.

'My brother said he'll put me up.'

'Excellent. Will work have you back?'

'No. I've been dismissed.'

'It's lucky Peterborough is such a thriving place. The fastest growing city in England. Or is that Milton Keynes?'

'Look, is this necessary? I got eighteen years.'

His face fell.

'Ah, sorry. I thought it was months.' He drummed his fingers on the table and then stood. 'I'll see you in eight years, then. Wait here, your offender manager has arrived. I'll send him in.'

I waited with my back to the door.

'Eighteen! Nice to see you again.'

Now, it was my face that dropped. It was the idiot from Reception, who booked me in after sentencing.

'You can imagine my joy when I got assigned your case, having met you when I was helping out in Reception.'

He sat opposite. No pen, no paper, just an inquisitive expression.

'Do you know what an offender manager does?'

'No.'

'It's my job to complete a report on you so we can transfer you out of here. This is a local jail to receive people from court and to manage short sentences. We aren't set up to look after inmates who have decades to serve. I need to ascertain your risk levels. Therefore, I have to understand your thinking and motivations. We will have quite a few chats over the next few months, starting now.'

'Okay.'

'Let's start at the beginning. Why did you do it?'

'I didn't.'

He leaned back in his seat. A smile came that didn't meet his eyes.

'I've been doing this for years. I've had murderers, rapists and arsonists in my care. People from all walks of life. I read your case file. What I've learnt in my time is that men convicted of terrifying offences like yours rarely admit to what they've done. At least not at the beginning.

'Let me guess, she was at your house, but you never touched her. She was lonely and vulnerable and you were just helping out. You don't know why a twelve-year-old would make up those accusations but she was damaged. You don't hold any malice for her as she was confused. Am I close?'

The smug shit was spot on.

'Yes.'

'Yet, in the end, you went guilty. Even though you knew you would get a heavy sentence. Scared to go to trial; to stand in court and deny it all? Didn't want to make a poor girl experience the trauma of cross-examination?'

'Yes.'

'I think you're guilty. The judge did too. Your barrister didn't even provide any character references. Looks like your friends didn't believe you either. You were in her bed by your own admission. Don't you know that's wrong? Whether your hands roamed under those sheets or not is just a matter of how mistaken you were.'

'I didn't do the things she said I did. It was her mother's boyfriend.'

'Really? Why aren't the police questioning him?'

'He's dead.'

'Very convenient. We wouldn't want him denying it either.'

He shook his head as he stood.

'I can see you aren't going to admit to the charges. Not today, anyway. You have many long nights with your own company over the next nine years. I believe it's the guilt that breaks people and finally makes them confess. Who knows, maybe it's boredom.

'Understand this. If you don't admit to what you did, then how can we rehabilitate you? We can't lower your risk profile if you can't see the error of your ways. We will want to see remorse, guilt and shame first. Then we can discuss how to stop these awful events occurring again. Otherwise you'll always be high risk and will never leave maximum security prisons. No cushy open jails for you. No working in the garden or popping home at the weekends. You will do hard time.'

It didn't feel like prison on our wing. Except for Kilkenny, most people were polite. We had vicars, teachers, airline pilots, police officers, prison officers, doctors, you name it.

Sex offenders take many forms. There was even a carpenter – who, as you could imagine, was the orderly at the wood workshop where I took a course. I tried to keep busy, and started to make a bench. There wasn't any rush.

On the day Doc left, I had my first cell search. It was a degrading experience. Two officers came in our cell.

'Your cell has been targeted for a cell spin. We will begin with a strip search and then we'll examine your entire room. Do you have any unauthorised items or anything illegal?'

Doc left the room and the two officers stood in front of me and put blue plastic disposable gloves on.

'Any religious or legal items you want us to be aware of?'

'No.'

'Anything that could hurt me or my colleague?'

'No.'

'Remove your T-shirt, please, and pass it here.'

I did. He searched it and handed it back.

'Put that back on and remove your trousers and socks.'

I did.

'And your pants. Turn around.'

Humiliated, I bent over. The two of them collapsed with laughter.

'Whoa there, tiger. It's a bit early for any of that.'

The other one tried to choke his amusement back, yet still couldn't resist adding to the mirth.

'I'll go to the seaside if I want to see starfish.'

They were a regular comedy duo.

'You want anything so bad you need to keep it up there, then it's yours.'

Still sniggering they sent me onto the wing to wait. They found nothing and, judging by the fact most of our stuff was where it was beforehand, they didn't search very hard either.

They'd watched TV as our channel had been changed, and it smelt like they'd had a cigarette. Doc reckoned they'd eaten some of his biscuits.

When they left, they handed Doc a big plastic bag.

'You're being transferred. HMP Whatton. The bus leaves in an hour. You will be packed and on it.'

After they left, I questioned Doc.

'Don't they give you any more notice than that if you're moving prisons?'

'No, sometimes they don't even give you an hour. If you've been troublesome, they just drag you on the transfer vehicle and your belongings follow at a later, non-specified, date. If you're lucky.'

It was strange to be so worthless.

'Where's Whatton?'

'Nottinghamshire. They call it the Paedo Palace as it's a whole jail full of sex offenders. It's okay. I've been there before.'

I helped him pack. We didn't fill the bag. I walked with him to the gates and shook his hand. It was lunchtime by that point, so everyone queued up by the shutters. A lot of prisoners wished him good luck. As he was marched off, I wondered at that. He'd done despicable things in his time, yet here he was a popular guy. Without him there, I felt vulnerable.

I walked back to my cell to get my plate and bowl. Someone was looking out of my window when I stepped inside. Kilkenny turned around and gave me an evil grin. He shoved past me but stopped at the door.

'I like Mars bars.'

The door swung shut and I remembered the offender manager's words. He was right. I would do hard time after all.

39

2010 – AGED 44

Clara came to visit me on the first day of August. I had to blink to make sure it was her. She'd spent the summer in the sun. Although she must have been cooling in the fountain of youth as she looked ten years younger. She was back to a normal size and seemed relaxed, even smiling at me when I approached her seat. It was a surreal moment.

When I got close to her, it seemed impossible that she was once mine, to love and to cherish. All the feelings from when we first dated, which had been forgotten, remained. My heart lurched as, yet again, I thought of the life I could have had.

I sat opposite and our eyes met. Mine dropped and I found myself looking at her hands, which she clasped on her lap. I had a strong urge to touch them. To feel someone else's warmth. They were so near, but I knew those hands might as well be behind a window.

Once again, I remembered all the opportunities when I could have held her and never did. I realised that it would be many years before I would be close to another person.

Prison had been my home for two years by that point. I'd

received a letter from Clara saying which days she could come and I'd booked the visit. It had been a long wait for that day to arrive. I let her start the talking as there was unlikely to be any interesting news from me. There would be nothing good from her either. She had written to tell me she was coming to say goodbye.

'How are you, Vinnie?'

'Fine, thank you.'

I wished people would stop asking that. They didn't want to know the truth. I felt like a flower, wilting through lack of sunlight and water. If I didn't get the things I needed to survive it would be too late to save me.

'Thank you for seeing me. I didn't want to just disappear, even after what happened. I'm going to get everything off my mind first and then, well, if you want to go back to your cell, then that's okay.'

'Go for it, Clara.'

She paused and then looked blank.

'God, I don't know where to start.'

'Anywhere is fine.'

'I don't think you deserved all those years. People have killed and been given less time.'

She stopped to wipe a solitary tear away.

'I also had a visit from Kirsty's mum, Michelle. She wanted money. Said that you owed her for what you did to her child. She was crazy when she came over, like she was on a different planet. I had to ring the police and they took her away. They also took Kirsty away. I heard she's been taken into care. I only saw Michelle once after that when she collected her stuff. There's a rumour going around that they found drugs at her house and she got sent to prison.'

'I haven't seen her.'

She stopped talking and laughed loudly. She struggled a

while to recover her senses. A release of tension, I supposed. People didn't seem to laugh like that in prison. I wasn't sure exactly what these walls took from you but the ability to be carefree was something you missed.

'Ahh, Vinnie. Where did it all go wrong?'

We both leaned back in our seats and considered those words. It was babies, or the lack of them. That said, other couples survived not having children. Although perhaps not ones who needed them as much as Clara. Maybe I should have wanted them as desperately as she did and we would have suffered the hopes and failures in a more united way. I tried to be strong when I should have been weak.

'I never seemed to be able to talk about everything properly.'

'Don't beat yourself up about that, Vinnie. What happened would have broken most relationships. For a long time, I was elsewhere. I knew you were there for me, at home, and I'm grateful for that. Yet, I think I lost my sanity. The miscarriages I had in the house, I kept one of them. Did you know that?'

I shook my head. Surely a good husband would have been aware. Her voice dropped to a whisper.

'I kept it in the jewellery box. The first time, I flushed it away in disgust but then I wanted it back. It was gone, too late, and there was nothing I could do. I would cry for hours with guilt and despair. So, I kept the second one. I would hold it.

'It was just a small bag really with a lump in it, yet sometimes it helped and other times I felt strange and morbid. I couldn't get any peace, or still my mind except when I was eating. I suppose I was mad. You put up with me when many would have left. I must have been awful to live with. I never blamed you, Vinnie. Only myself and my father.'

'No, you—'

'Shush now. I need to finish. My father raped me. That's

where that STD came from. I finally told my mum what happened and she believed him instead of me. That's why they never visited our flat. I felt crazy and that's what she said I was.'

'Why didn't you tell the police?'

'He was my father and I didn't want him to go to prison.'

'Yet you let me go to prison.'

'When I told him to stop, he did. I told you and you carried on.'

'I didn't do it.'

'That's what he said. He was convincing too. You doubt yourself and I was there. I don't know precisely what you did. You did do something wrong though and you're being punished. I hope that girl is safe now.'

Another small piece of me died as I realised she would never be able to look at me in the same way again, whatever I said. She continued, her voice getting stronger with each word.

'My father dropped down dead not long after you were sent here. Heart failure was better than he deserved. I hope they saved an unpleasant fiery pit for him. Without you to help me, I had a complete breakdown: screaming, shouting – a total stereotype. I was hospitalised and that was my rock bottom.

'They gave me therapy and support for all the things that had happened. They taught me that what I'd done was nothing to be ashamed of. That I was normal. My mum came to see me and apologised too. All of a sudden, my compulsion to overeat vanished. One of the male nurses took a shine to me and, well, we began dating.'

She sensed me stiffening in my seat but continued. Brutal. Each word bumping into my heart.

'I live with him now. We're going to foster in the future. I will have my children, Vinnie. Be sure of that. I want to get married again too, so I suppose I'm here for a divorce.'

What can you say to that? I couldn't think of a response. I was the man slumped at the stake after the firing squad had filled its purpose.

'This is closure, for us both. Look what we did to each other. We can still have a life, just not together. I'm afraid I associate you with so many bad things and I want to move forward. I hope, with enough distance, I could perhaps remember you fondly. But I have to say goodbye.'

Surprisingly, there were tears for neither of us. They'd been shed. She stayed for a few minutes longer but we could both see there was little point in continuing. I wished her the best. She hadn't done wrong and maybe now she could get what she deserved.

She gathered her things together and stood before me. This time it was me that held her gaze until she looked away. With a wry expression, she made her way to the back of the visit hall and nodded to the officer, who unlocked the door and escorted her out. I sat forward in my seat, head in hands, tired.

'What are you waiting for, Roach? Get up and get a move on, or your next visit will be with a dentist.'

That year was a tough one. The only respite from Kilkenny's never-ending bullying was a letter from my brother saying he'd received a cheque for thirty thousand pounds from Clara. My share of the winnings, less some expenditure. I clung to that like a drowning man thrown a rope. That money was my future. With it, I had a chance.

I knew I wasn't the only person on the wing who was suffering Kilkenny's reign because many an inmate sported random bruises and limps. As if we were all forced to play a ferocious sport each night and suffered the next day. Oddly, it wasn't the violence that drained your soul, it was the hopelessness and vulnerability. It consumed every moment.

The industrial kitchens in the prison used to cook the food and send it to the wings for distribution by the wing workers out of the servery. Kilkenny used to wander in and help himself to what he fancied, even though there was only enough for each man. Someone always went short.

On the odd occasion, an officer would catch him and tell him to clear off, but he was sneaky and knew the staff had other concerns. As far as they could see, it progressed smoothly because no one complained.

Every Saturday morning, they gave us a fry-up for lunch. Sausages, bacon, hash browns, beans and a boiled egg. It was the high point of the week for many. As I said, in prison you focus on the small things. I saw a man cry when Kilkenny took his sausages. He didn't eat them, just threw them in the bin.

Once, I saw Kilkenny with his face buried in the large servery fridge as I passed the open door. I found myself wandering in. He was unaware I was there but the aggression I occasionally felt was gone. I imagined kicking his backside and then slamming the door on his head, many times, perhaps while laughing.

However, I left, before he saw me, and spent the next few weeks trying to think of a reason why I hadn't done it.

40

2011 – AGE: 45

I thought my life would never change, and then my transfer came through. HMP Wakefield, or, as it's affectionately known, the 'Monster Mansion'. Over seven hundred of the worst rapists, perverts and murderers behind many bleak walls. Nevertheless, if it got me away from Kilkenny, I was happy to go.

It felt odd to have been somewhere so long and have so few good memories. The problem was they were running out of spaces for men like me as the number of historic sex offences convictions was increasing exponentially. On a daily basis, they brought new shell-shocked residents to our wing. Fresh poison each week. I would help those who asked, as Doc had looked after me.

My run of bad luck continued. As I held my breath in the enclosed compartment on the van, I heard the others groan when a heavy step with a familiar voice came on board.

'Who wants to share a cell with me, then?'

I guess that was why it was a family motto. I'd had the opportunity to take revenge on Kilkenny, yet I didn't do what had to be done.

* * *

The gods finally answered one of my prayers and they sent me to a different wing from Kilkenny. I later heard, through my cleaning job, that his business was thriving at his new home, too. Nasty for them. As a jail, I preferred it over Peterborough as everyone was in for something sick, therefore few were judgemental. There was still the occasional flash of horrific violence, which ensured you remained vigilant.

There were men with whole life sentences who would never get out, but the majority had minimum tariffs. For example, twenty years. I always thought these people would have nothing to lose and their behaviour would reflect that.

However, inmates knew parole boards would go back to the start of the sentence when they were deciding if you were fit for life in the community twenty years down the line. If you hadn't behaved, then you weren't released. Twenty years could easily become twenty-five. Therefore, after an initial settling-in period where a long sentence might render you temporarily insane, most prisoners turned themselves off and, like recovering alcoholics, got through one day at a time.

That was what I did. I hadn't killed anyone so I would be let go at the halfway point regardless and, amongst some of these men, I almost felt lucky. Imagine being sent to jail at twenty-five, knowing you would be sixty when you got out. Possibly due to a single moment of madness. It was no wonder some chose the quick way out.

I only had one visit whilst I was at HMP Wakefield: my brother. He came once as I asked him not to bother after that. It was a long drive for him and I was unsettled afterwards. Frank reminded me there was a world out there that I was missing out on.

He tried to keep it low-key and not say too much, yet I could picture him drinking ice cold beer in gardens or strolling out in the open. I pined for the normality of not having to share a home with so many men.

It was good to see him too and he came with fantastic news. He and Silent Kevin had repaired my Porsche and sold it for ten thousand pounds. It wasn't the money that was empowering this time, it was that Kevin had done something for me.

I told Frank I would love it if Kevin visited. He said he would ask. He also let me know that he had checked our family tree and we had numerous villains in our ancestry. That was not so encouraging.

It was around this time that I kept dreaming about running. It wasn't a nightmare whilst I slept, as I felt alive. It was the sinking horror on waking that made me feel entombed. As soon as my eyes closed, I could picture myself jogging on a beach. I would go faster and faster, leaving light footsteps in the sand. Instead of tiring, it was as if I were young and unbreakable. Almost like flying. The body in motion, alive and healthy. I would wake in the middle of the night drenched in sweat and my sheets tangled.

Then, I slowly discovered that I was still locked in a small room. The heavy fetid air in the cell suppressed my breathing, but it was despair that crushed me.

However, a tiny part of me rejoiced that, for at least some of the day, I had been free.

41

2012 – AGE: 46

An unexpected feature of being incarcerated was that if they transferred you a long way from home, once a year, you could return to your local jail for accumulated visits. It was not unusual for inmates to have no one to come and see them if they were moved ten miles away, never mind over a hundred like I had gone. In that case, your visits built up and you 'went home' so you could stay in touch with family and friends.

An officer explained it was all down to rehabilitation and reoffending. Inmates, and men in particular, would shut themselves off from anyone who knew them. When their release date arrived, they were all alone in the world. Sleeping rough and feeling neglected by society was a sure way to return to criminal ways, even if it was just stealing food. The best place for most after they left was with their loved ones. Maintaining relationships was key.

I booked both Silent Kevin and Frank in on the same visit. I didn't know you could do that either until someone kindly explained. While Frank went to get the cakes, Kevin opened up.

'I'm sorry, Vinnie.'

'I'm not sure you have anything to feel bad for.'

'That's not true. I wasn't a good friend.'

'I bet it was a lot to take in.'

'It was. I was worried what people might say, you know, about sticking up for you, or even coming to visit. I thought they would think I was one too.'

He didn't need to say the word paedophile. Yet, its presence sat between us.

'I didn't do it, Kevin.'

'You got eighteen years. I read the news. It was all over the papers.'

'I was guilty of some things, stuff I shouldn't have done, but I didn't rape her or have sex with her.'

As the words come out, I realised how hollow they sounded. Was this also a confession of sorts? My offender manager told me three years ago that I would eventually want to confess – to everything.

'Vinnie. You don't need to try to explain. I can't begin to understand what happened and nor do I want to. We all do awful things. I've made mistakes myself and I hope that my friends wouldn't desert me, like I did you. You've been punished, let's leave it at that.'

I wondered whether he would have supported me back then, had I stuck to my story. Kevin's character reference would certainly have bolstered my confidence, if not my chances. Him not answering my letters and calls at the time weighed heavy on me. Each day with no reply was another shovel full of dirt on my chest.

Frank returned and put down the drinks.

'Look, they had decent-looking cakes. Cheap too.' He sensed the gloom. 'You both all right?'

'Yeah,' Kevin said. 'It's just a shame they didn't let me bring in my beers.'

As we chuckled, that was the start of me thinking I could do my nine years. Maybe when I left, something of me would have persevered, and I'd have a place to return to. 'Ride your bang-up,' the young scrotes used to shout as their friends were dragged to the block after trying to distract each other from their pointless existences. I would ride my bang-up and perhaps I would survive.

* * *

Each day blended into the next. I recognised others rotating around the country's prison estate, like a tour of duty for the morally challenged. While these people wouldn't become friends, it was nice to see a familiar face. Sometimes you'd chat, like you'd bumped into each other walking your dogs at the local park.

A man on the last day of his sentence explained that I would still look forward to getting out. He had been in jail for nearly thirty years. I couldn't help but ask him.

'Did you do it?'

'What they said? I suppose so. There are shades and perspectives but I was guilty. Who isn't? A man told me not to get involved in the prison culture when I got here, and that saved me. That was good advice because it's all fake. Go to the gym, get yourself fit, learn a trade or help others. Try to eat healthily and give something for nothing. Do those things and your future might be your own.'

He regarded me as he must have done many men over such a long period.

'You can't change the past, only what lies ahead. On a lighter note, you know what's the craziest thing about this whole experience?'

'Go on.'

'I'm out tomorrow, Monday, at 9 a.m. I will walk through those doors and within reason I can do what I want, after thirty years of being told what I can and can't do. Yet, all the time I've spent here has folded in on itself. It feels like I came here on Friday.'

42

2013 – AGE: 47

Instead of going back to the Monster Mansion, they transferred me to the seaside. HMP Albany, or HMP Isle of Wight as it's now known. I couldn't see the sea from my cell and the place still smelt how you'd expect, so the basics were the same. Some said the gulls drove them crazy, cawing away at memories of better times.

The jail housed approximately 1,100 inmates who the Ministry of Justice described as being 'vulnerable sex offenders'. It was a strange world. At one point, I thought they were mixing male and female prisoners together before someone politely told me they were cross-dressers.

There were two on our wing. Phoenix was ever so friendly and used to come into my cell to borrow things. She, as she asked me to call her, was a jittery being but remarkably like a girl.

She was extremely popular. I never asked about her 'friends' but, judging by her make-up and constant supply of cigarettes, they were generous. She got a bit of grief from men calling her Tranny and She-male but she laughed it off good-heartedly. She said she liked being my friend because I didn't ask for anything.

Phoenix used to tell the same joke over and over again. Q: 'What's the difference between a cross-dresser and a transsexual?' A: 'Two years.' She was a force of nature as opposed to the other 'lady', Georgie, who was just a force: mass times acceleration.

Georgie had the body, strength and demeanour of a recently made-redundant coal miner. She scared me rigid, and the staff too. Maybe she did it to fuck with them, who knows, but it worked.

I suspect she might not have been fully committed as she often lay on her bed watching sport and put garish lipstick and eye shadow on just for association. It was quite a thing to watch a hairy eighteen-stone man in full make-up slam pool balls down with a strength that made your ears ring.

Only one man tried to bully Phoenix when I was there. The next morning, we all stood in our doorways and watched as Georgie left her cell and let herself into his. There wasn't any noise, and I never did hear what happened, but I have to say it was the quietest and safest wing that I'd ever been on. I was almost sad to leave when the time came.

They got me a job in Reception, talking to the new inmates about what they could expect from their custodial stay. I enjoyed it and found a sense of purpose I never had while I worked in the factory.

Many were still in denial and kept asking about appeals and timescales. I hadn't seen a single successful appeal apart from a few where the sentence was reduced. A few even had their sentences increased for wanton waste of the court's time when there wasn't any fresh evidence. It wasn't surprising, I supposed, that there was no appetite amongst the judiciary to cast doubt on their fellows' judgements.

For most, the hardest part of prison was accepting that you had little control over your day. If you had a long sentence, and I saw many men at the wrong end of a time period that they would need decent health and good fortune to see out, the soundest advice was forget about your old life. Tough love for new arrivals. Not what they would want to hear, but wise.

Unusually, prison is one of the only parts of society where the poor, the unloved and especially those who have nothing, get the better end of the deal. If you have spouses, children, ageing parents, or unattended businesses, prison is akin to being sent to hell.

They assigned me a new offender manager. He was all business. He explained again that he couldn't downgrade my risk if I didn't accept I was guilty of those distant crimes. Could it have been true? I didn't remember much by then. In a quiet moment, he told me to play the game. When I queried this, he replied with a smile.

'Just say you did those things and you are full of remorse. No one else need know. It'll be your little secret. You may even end up in a nice D-cat prison.'

Hardly inspiring, hearing it from the staff. It might have made our meetings more fruitful and longer though. I'd heard other prisoners say similar things but the time for confessing was long past. A part of me wished I'd gone to trial and had my day in court. At least then, everything would have been out in the open.

Even though I kept busy, I retained an undercurrent of restlessness. I, too, pined for my old life, despite my advice to others. I still carried round an unbalancing sensation of feeling I shouldn't be inside. Maybe everyone felt like that. No one would come along now and tell me it was all a big mistake and I could go home. That point had disappeared years back.

I remembered the old lady from the Hotel De Paris saying, 'Embrace life. The part that matters is over before you know it.' She was right. I would be fifty-one when I got out. Was that too late? Although if I asked a sixty-year-old, he would no doubt tell me I was a young man and had the rest of my days ahead of me.

I also had my first alcoholic drink for five years. An inmate called Pew asked me to read a letter he'd received from home. I followed him into his cell and sat on his bed. He must have easily been eighty years old. I smiled and waited as he got a folder out and shuffled through the letters, one by one.

He was the type who kept his cell pristine. Every Saturday he would borrow the mop and brush and make a big show of it. He was nice enough, a little over-friendly but harmless, with an ill-fitting pair of false teeth.

They moved of their own accord as he talked. Clicking and slurping. I found it very hard to focus on anything else whenever I spoke to him. It wasn't only that they seemed to have a life of their own, it was just incongruous to be staring at perfectly formed teeth on such a wizened face. Still, he was good for a smoke if you ran out and I don't think he cared whether you listened or not.

'Here it is.'

He passed me a yellowing envelope with a thick letter in it. He noticed me looking at the front where there was no stamp and it was addressed to Lenny Harris.

'It was handed in for me, by the girlfriend.'

A strange thought ran through me as I prayed to any God ever to have existed that there wouldn't be any filth in it.

'You sure? I don't want to intrude on your privacy.'

'I can't read it myself, the writing's too small. To be honest, I can barely see the TV nowadays. That's why they call me Pew.'

He paused as his words hit home.

'Ah, I get it. The vicious, deadly, blind beggar from *Treasure Island*. Nice nickname.'

Lenny laughed, an unusual deep open-mouthed laugh, and had to scramble around on the bed to stop his teeth falling out.

'None of that sex talk in there, young man, if that's what you're worried about. If you want pictures, you'll have to pay extra.'

As we chuckled together, I realised it was moments like these, on an idle Sunday, that made jail endurable.

'Drink?'

'Erm, I'm okay, thanks.'

I was dubious of old people's consumables ever since May from next door experimented on us with her mouldy stuff. He must have been deaf as well as blind because he plonked a plastic cup full of orange juice in front of me. Inmates never refused free-bies and juice was something I didn't spend my own money on, so I picked it up with enthusiasm.

'Steady with that, it's got a lotta oompah loompa.'

As it came towards my mouth, a stench of rotten corpses snaked up my nose like the branches from an evil tree. If zombies wore underwear that would be how it'd smell.

I'd heard of hooch but, seeing as I had never drunk much outside those walls, there seemed little point in imbibing while inside them. It must have been the British in me, as, even though an entire lifetime's worth of instinct told me not to, I took a sip. My eyes squinted and, despite my best efforts, closed.

It hit my stomach in the same way I imagined drinking petrol would. The aftertaste was so foul, when I spoke it made my front teeth protrude.

'Nice,' I managed.

'Isn't it? They say it's my best yet. Now, read that letter. I miss my girl.'

The contents were pretty standard but it went on and on. What she had for breakfast, what she liked on TV, who came to see her, what the weather was doing, a blow-by-blow account of her closest friend's urinary infection that was enlightening and horrifying in equal measure, and finally an entire page on whether she should cut down on caffeine or not. She chose not to.

It was so mind-blowingly boring that I found myself sipping the foul liquid as I spoke. I was amazed it didn't start to taste better as my brain furred up, but each new sip was a fresh crime.

Lenny, or Pew, or whatever he was called, stared at me as I read in morbid fascination as though I were revealing the location of a lost treasure. He sipped water from a bottle when I'd almost got to the end and nodded, letting me know all was right with the world.

'You not having any of your delicious beverage?'

'What, that stuff? No, not for years. Gives me the shits. Real bad.'

I'd finished the large cup twice during my reading. He'd kindly topped it up on the odd occasion too. My lower bowel shuddered as though a train had gone through it. I stood to leave and found I couldn't stand straight. I needed to get back to my cell. Quickly.

'It ends with, "See you in a few days, Sailor. I'll be ready with some lovin'. Love Louisa".'

As I peered down at him through watering vision, I noted the sides of his mouth drop.

'You out soon?' I managed as a growl came from my bowels that would have pleased a T-Rex.

'Yes, a few days.' His eyes took on a far-off look.

I didn't have time for more pleasantries to find out why that wasn't good news as platform two had an imminent arrival. It was coming fast and wouldn't be stopping for passengers. The gurgle that came from near my sphincter would have caused concern on the Isle of Wight ferry as it sounded like the plaintive distress call of a wounded whale.

Lenny raised his eyes at me.

'You're a brave man, drinking that much. You kids crack me up.'

He passed me a pack of two toilet rolls.

'Here, I should say you'll be needing them.'

I crept out of his cell in a crouching style that, even in my frightened state, made me think of the Pink Panther. My back hugged the wall; I knew if anyone touched me the fallout would be nuclear. I almost wept when I got to my cell with my honour intact.

I stood in front of the throne and yanked my trousers and pants down in a swift move and sat down. The propulsion behind the emission was so powerful it actually raised me up and I shouted, 'Argghhhhh.' The toilet rolls were needed.

The next day I looked decidedly ropey. I'd had little sleep and had to ask the nurse for cream for my exhausted rear end. The guy in the queue next to me queried my haunted features.

'You look rough, mate.'

'I was in Lenny's cell yesterday afternoon.'

Once he'd stopped laughing and wiped his face, which took nearly a minute, he explained.

'That mischievous old git still up to his tricks, I see.'

'What do you mean?'

'His hooch really works, but there's a harsh price to pay for being tipsy. He's always giving it to people he doesn't know. One guy shit himself in the visit hall last month. Those who know Pew, and most do, won't touch it.'

'What's he in for?'

'You'd imagine something harmless, wouldn't you? He killed two kids about fifty years ago. I'm not sure of the details, I think they were sixteen or thereabouts. He got life with a minimum of thirty-five years. Did he get you to read the letter he just received?'

'Yes, from Louisa.'

'Louisa was a pen pal who wrote to him for years. She died the day before he got out. That letter's fifteen years old. I read it to him a few years back. He went mad when he was released after waiting all that time. He couldn't handle the conditions of his licence and the police picked him up near a school, so he got recalled to prison. If you're a lifer, you then have to prove you're fit to leave again.

'He did get out five years later but still couldn't handle it. He's been here ever since. I suspect he's gone crazy now. I don't think he knows she's dead, or, if he does, he just likes the company. So, we humour him and take it in turns to read the letter.

'Only the new arrivals drink the hooch though, and then only once.'

43

2014 – AGE 48

I accepted that I was there for another three years and made the most of it. The gym was the first port of call. Most people imagine prison gym as a bunch of shaven-headed ogres chucking weights around. I was in a sex offenders' jail so it was considerably different.

There were a lot of old men for a start, trying to battle the advance of osteoarthritis and Alzheimer's. There was the odd muscle-bound individual like Kilkenny but the rest were often kids with no idea. I used to enjoy looking at them as they returned to the wing – walking funny and all pumped up, despite their sloppy form and lack of progress.

I just got down to it. Focus on the weight and repetitions and you could forget, for, at least, a while, where you were. When you're young, you exercise with vigour and enthusiasm, thinking you will look like body builders, even though you won't. When you're old, life has taught you differently, so what you're really aiming for is damage limitation. So you don't look too bad. That's not as motivational. Still, I stuck with it and found some peace as my body grew and strengthened.

As with all parts of prison life, there was violence. The worst beating I saw was for an old pervert who didn't go to do any exercise at all but was always having a shower when the gym posse returned. They would rush in to get clean in the final few minutes before being locked in for the night.

He'd be there. Slow eyes on young bodies. Most prisoners lack common sense but many aren't stupid. I could still smell blood in the communal showers the next day.

Frank was dating again. New girlfriend, same slurred problems. The last time I rang him, I could hear the shouting in the background.

'What the hell is that racket?'

'It's Lynsey.'

'Is she on fire?'

'Very funny. She saw an email from an old friend and thinks I'm cheating on her.'

'Are you?'

'No. Not yet, anyway. I've made a bit of a mistake moving in with her and I am not looking forward to the leaving conversation.'

'Have you got another nutter on your hands?'

'Do you know what, Vinnie? She was fine, it's me that's messed her up. I seem to get bored and give up. That slowly drives them to dark places. I'm comparing all relationships to Mum and Dad's, even though I now think theirs was twisted.'

He stopped talking as the shouting came closer. There seemed to be some kind of tussle with the phone, followed by more bad language. Obviously, I had time to spare, so I waited.

He'd moved to Hertfordshire with her. I couldn't remember where. Things like that weren't important to a man like me. I wouldn't be going there or meeting her, so the information flowed in and out.

We all said that. Our own weird bubble was all we knew. I doubted they'd be together when I got out anyway. One of the nasty parts about being a sex offender is you usually don't get to leave and go where you like at the end of your sentence. You are likely to have to live in an approved premises first, where you have to prove again that you aren't a danger. Like a hotel for 'wrong'uns,' with more hoops to jump through.

When he finally picked the phone back up, he was breathing hard.

'So, how's prison?'

'Frank, can't you try harder? Be nice to her?'

'Sure, Vinnie. I'll try. Just sometimes I wonder if there's something rotten running through our family.'

That wasn't a convincing committal. He had more news to tell me though. Some of a delicate nature.

'Vinnie, that girl who said those things about you is in prison.'

'Really, what for?'

'A range of stuff, shoplifting mostly. Reading between the lines she was a prostitute too.'

The words didn't seem real. It was hard to attach them to the quiet girl who changed our lives. I knew I would feel desperately sad when I had time to process the facts. She couldn't have been more than twenty. I refused to think who was to blame.

'I'm going to the gym now. Three times a week, sometimes more. Enhanced prisoners can go more or less when they like.'

Frank didn't care I'd changed the subject.

'That's a good idea. Keep your mind busy?'

'I've volunteered to be a listener too.'

'What's a listener?'

'The listener scheme is a peer support service, which aims to reduce suicide and self-harm in prisons. Samaritan volunteers select, train and support prisoners to become listeners. Listeners provide confidential emotional support to their fellow inmates who are struggling to cope.'

'What does all that guff mean?'

'I'm not sure, I just read it off a leaflet to you. The general idea is that when the prisoners want to speak to someone, they call a listener.'

''Don't you need training?'

'They give you some beforehand. It's not about giving advice, it's about being there in a non-judgemental way.'

'So, you have to listen to other people have a moan. What do you get out of it?'

'The ability to help others. It's lonely here. The nights can last for years when you only have your mistakes for company.'

'Yes, very poetic. Sounds to me that they need to man up, not sob to you.'

'I knew you'd understand.'

If you haven't been to prison, it's hard to get your head round the feeling of worthlessness. You drag dark emotions round like a contagious cold, infecting those you come into contact with. The opportunity to do something positive, for yourself and others, is tempting.

Frank, of all people, wouldn't get that. As those thoughts entered my mind, I remembered all the years that Frank had been at my side. After everything. We rarely know ourselves, so it's only natural that even close family can be a mystery but I couldn't say that he was a bad person.

I changed the subject again.

'Do you recall much about when we were young?'

His pause was too short, as if he was expecting the question. Surely, it was a yes or no answer.

'Some.'

'I remember nothing before the accident. That's not normal. I was nearly seven years old then.'

'Nothing at all?'

'No, I have strange dreams, almost like flashbacks.'

'Like what?'

'There was one where there are kids on a slide and one won't let the other off. We're there. Did that happen?'

This time the pause is long. The response measured.

'There was an incident, not long before your accident. You were on a slide and I was waiting. A kid couldn't get off. Another boy was bullying him, making him stay up there. It wasn't until he had been up there ages and he'd pissed himself that he was let down. That's a strange thing to remember. Anything else?'

As I spoke again, the sounds of female shouting came back and this time the phone went dead. I poured myself a cup of tea in my cell, put my feet up to watch the news, and wondered if things could be worse even if you were free.

44

They accepted me on the listener programme and I received my training. I was buoyed by my successes and became upbeat. Another con noticed and took me down a peg or two. 'You only begin to enjoy it here when you've forgotten what the other options are.' I suspect the few moments before that conversation were the zenith of my prison career as gradually, almost imperceptibly, it began to go wrong.

The way it worked in our jail was if someone requested a listener, the prison staff would come to your cell and ask you to do it. If it was after bang-up then they escorted you past all the closed doors. I don't know why but I enjoyed that part of it. Maybe thinking I was better than the rest. It was strange to imagine each box containing a damaged life.

The first few times, I went with an experienced listener and just listened myself. I wasn't opinionated so I found it simple. The idea was that you asked open questions, like 'how did that make you feel?', 'what could you have done differently?', or just said nothing. Many wanted to rant and rage, or sob and cry, without any interaction or help. They just didn't want to do it alone.

It sounded easy but for some it was impossible. A few blokes on my course couldn't stop giving their views. Wife's cheating on you: then leave her. Son's a junkie: chuck him out and cut him loose. Someone has mugged you off: fuck that, I don't take shit from anyone.

Their lack of self-awareness was amusing. No doubt their forthright nature was one of the main reasons they had been removed from society in the first place. Even if you wanted to receive advice, it would be best not to get it from men like them.

All my accompanied calls were pretty simple prison stuff. Thoughts of self-harm or suicide abounded, and it was astounding to think having another human being there to listen to their problems was often enough to help those feelings pass. It was a sex offenders' wing so many didn't want to mention their crimes, which was fine by me.

One guy just cried and cried, for about an hour. At the end, he stood up, wiped his eyes and shook my hand the way a vicar does as you leave church. I saw him in Reception a few weeks after, where he gave me a warm smile and said, 'Thank you.' I later found out he had been selling naked pictures of his children on the Internet.

I began to have my doubts about the role. That man had seemed remarkably normal – pleasant even. I sat and thought about what he had done and the pity drained from me like tears from the newly bereaved. As I did the job longer, inmates opened up. They gave me presents afterwards, a radio once, and I became a somebody. Even something in nothing was progress.

However, the things I heard would melt stone. Horrific, sick, desperate crimes, committed against the vulnerable and unwary. I knew for certain there were sicker men than me in this world and I helped them all. I also understood the contempt people like us received. We were all the same. Just one big disgusting danger to society.

The staff recognised my skills and would use me regularly in the hope of avoiding an incident. I feared for my soul as it was fed graphic details of the worst that one human could do to another. I wilted. Sometimes officers would regard me with strange looks as I left another quiet man. What had I become? But it was curiosity, not sympathy. The trust bestowed in me made me feel normal, but I wasn't.

The final listens I did were severe. I was going back to HMP Peterborough for accumulated visits. My brother hadn't answered his phone for a few weeks, but Silent Kevin said they had agreed to come together again. On my last evening before the move they woke me at 3 a.m. A man was repeatedly smashing his head against the cell door whenever he was left alone. If I couldn't calm him, he would need to be sedated.

'What have I done? What have I done?'

'Perhaps you could tell me.'

I gave him a smile, even though his forehead seeped blood onto his screwed-up face. He had pulled off any kind of bandage they had tried to cover him with.

'We were happy. I didn't understand why she needed space. I went to see her and I don't know what came over me. I had to have her one more time.'

A familiar need behind these wire fences.

'It's a blur, really. I wasn't sure who was most surprised.'

Trust me, it was her.

'She began to scream. I panicked.'

Then, you did the unthinkable.

I left him sobbing but quietened. Was there a large part of me that wanted to tell him he was insignificant – that he had no value? Shout at him that he was less than nothing as he had done something that could never be undone?

There was, but we all had a job to do and I did mine. They taught me that no one was all bad. Everyone had qualities to offer the world, whatever they might have done. A smile, in a place like this, was a powerful thing.

The officers looked at me in awe as they escorted me to my cell. They were relaxed though, because it was such a regular occurrence. 'Sleep well,' they said as my door locked. I couldn't, in fact, hadn't been doing for quite some time. That was how I would be remembered: like him.

I wished I could have talked to Kirsty. Asked her why she'd said those things. I should have gone to court because I might as well have got twenty years as opposed to eighteen. If I had seen and heard her, I would have known if those terrible events ever occurred. I remembered telling her to keep our friendship between us. Secrets – what I now understood to be the currency of paedophiles.

I'd made a matchstick ashtray over many painstaking hours. I grabbed it and crushed it. There was an instant release of satisfaction and joy, but then sorrow straight after. A thing of beauty destroyed with one careless uncontrolled emotion.

Maybe that was how it was with these criminals. They understood evil urges were in their DNA and knew they should never let their inner desires see the light. Yet they surfaced, as the urge was too strong, too powerful for them to deny what was ultimately who they were.

Then, it was too late. Lives were ruined, people were dead, prisons were full.

The radio was my saviour through those quiet hours when I contemplated my existence. I flicked it on that depressing morning, and the past became present.

'It's just gone 4 a.m. on Isle of Wight Radio, so here's a little number with a little culture. It's "Vincent", by Don McLean.'

'Starry, starry night.'

The song went on and on. My happiness depleting with each word.

'You took your life, as lovers often do.'

I'd had long nights in prison. That was an eon. Sara had been far from my thoughts and then, with a song that I hadn't even known was sad, I was leaving on that bus again.

I wondered how her life had panned out. If she was happy, single, healthy, or maybe a parent. I allowed myself a few minutes of imagining, perhaps hoping, she thought of me. I remembered her saying I made her think of this song. Mad that I'd only ever heard it the odd time on the radio since, nearly thirty years later. Why hadn't I bought it? Perhaps I didn't care.

I believe that getting old is when the memories of your youth fade so you aren't sure what's real and what isn't. That's why you should stay in touch with the friends you had when you were young and keep on good terms with family. Even if that means biting down on your concerns.

Reminisce, it's free and is one of life's greatest gifts. Memories ground you so your future can fly. The torture of prison is wishing you were elsewhere, and that was what brought me down.

Over the next few months, something already damaged in me finally broke.

45

2015 – AGE 49

The scary thing about returning to my home town's prison was that it felt like nothing had changed. The staff were mostly the same and so were the clientele. As I sat in the waiting room in Reception, I saw the boy from next door to our flat, Ben, walk past.

If you are on the VP (Vulnerable Persons) wing they keep you separate from mainstream prisoners. That's where the term nonce comes from – Not On Normal Courtyard Exercise. Ben wasn't in uniform so he must have been an inmate too. I looked down, ashamed, as he stared in my direction.

As I was escorted to the house blocks, I also saw that idiot, Jake – the one who threw the golf ball through my window all those years ago. People needed protecting from him, but I felt sorry for Ben. He had little chance with his booze-hound parents, and with friends such as Jake, it was almost inevitable he would end up in a place like this.

The staff were well pleased when they found out I was now a listener. Worryingly, their previous one had attempted to kill himself a few weeks before he got out. I tried not to think too much of the implications of that.

They also offered me a plum role in Reception but I refused. For some reason, the reception orderly was always taken from the VP wing and spent most of the day making coffees and cheese toasties for the officers. It's hard to describe what a cheese toastie smells and tastes like if you have been denied that pleasure for years. If you worked hard, you often came away with excess sandwiches and crisps too that they left for the prisoners being let out on day release.

Nevertheless, I couldn't stand the thought of seeing anyone I knew if I worked there. It also made me finally accept that if I stayed in my home town, I could bump into those who would be aware I had signed the Sex Offenders Register. My life would never be normal again.

No wonder people couldn't face it. I took a job in the woodwork room again. I wanted to make a new ashtray to replace the one I destroyed. My lack of control worried me, and it reminded me of the terrible crimes that men here committed.

I wandered into the office on my first morning back on the wing. They had a whiteboard with all the prisoners' names on in cell order. I scanned down them and grinned. Cell six, Albert Gilroy. Doc. It would be nice to see a friendly face.

The officers opened all the doors at 7.15 in the morning whether you were awake or not. The kind ones shouted 'breakfast' through the gap because if you didn't get up, it was a long while until dinner. Doc's door was still ajar, but the lights weren't on inside. I pushed the door open and stepped in.

There was an unusual pungent aroma in the room that reminded me of bad times. The breathing, though, was slow and strong.

'Doc.'

He took a long time to wake and I had to repeat his name three or four times. He seemed bewildered. I was leaving when he spoke out.

'Vinnie, is that you?'

'Yes, Doc. It would be better to meet again in different circumstances but it's nice to see you well.'

It was a lie. He appeared drawn and sickly. The intelligence behind his eyes remained but he also looked furtive and trapped. He put out his hand, which I took, thinking he wanted help from his bed. Instead, he held it.

'Thank you for that but we both know it isn't true. I'm dying.'

'Aren't we all?'

I was trying to cheer him up, yet I just sounded glib.

'Cancer.'

'Where?'

'It would be quicker if I told you where it wasn't.'

'Is there hope?'

'None. Three or four months, more or less. Less probably. I should understand better than most. I'm scared, Vinnie.'

That was how he looked. I stared at the shrunken man on the bed before me and he was afraid. It would be dreadful to be a medical man and know exactly what lay ahead. I should think it better not to be aware and deal with the pain if and when it arrived.

I struggled with what to say. There were no platitudes for a diagnosis like that.

'How long a sentence did you get?'

'Twelve months.'

'I see.'

He choked on a laugh.

'How long are you here for?' he asked.

'Same sentence, remember? I'm actually back here for six

months. They have me on a variety of courses. Stop the Hurt is one. I might even be able to stay until I'm released now. It's only two years away.'

That news pleased him and he rested his head on the pillow.

'Can't you get compassionate leave, Doc? You know, released early.'

He pulled himself up, seemingly having to draw on reserves to do so.

'I hope they don't give me a compassionate release. I've got nowhere to go. They don't do that often and you have to be bed-bound, so I'm not too worried. It's not that dying in prison scares me, or the pain. I'm afraid of dying alone.'

'They'd put you in the ward, wouldn't they? I don't remember you going to chapel on a Sunday either.'

'Sure, when I'm too frail to look after myself I'll be put in a nappy by strangers. There will be no one to mop my brow when the time comes. It's weird, all the twisted things I've done and here I am – not wanting to leave without someone I know at my side. I really hope there isn't a God because if there is, I'm in the shit.'

His cold paper skin seemed to burn in my hand as I could see purpose in his comments. I was saved from replying by the bellowed, 'Breakfast is over, behind your doors.'

Ironically, it was the arrival of another old acquaintance that would keep me from doing what I suspected Doc wanted me to do.

46

They came after lunch and took me from the woodwork class. The nervous officer chattered on the way there but I had heard it so many times, I didn't listen. I knew what I had to do.

There was a walkway between the house blocks where we lived and the main educational part of the prison. If the weather was good, you could feel the sun beat down on your face. All the metal, and lack of wind due to the high walls, magnified the heat. As it warmed me, I often felt I could be anywhere.

It was a fleeting pleasure but a free one I could also enjoy when I was released. Sometimes, the prisoners would stop and bask with their faces turned up like lizards. Only the harshest officers wouldn't give the inmates a few seconds.

I was taken back to my wing and led to the single cells at the bottom. I could hear sobbing before his keys jangled. He led me in and I found my old nemesis, Mr Kilkenny. Incredibly, he didn't recognise me. The officer backed out of the door and locked it. His footsteps had receded to nothing before it registered I could be in danger. I wasn't. He wanted to confess and I would listen.

'I'd been off my head all night. Charlie and pills, vodka, shots, you name it. We went to an after party and it was the speed bombs that did it. Huge parts of the evening are missing. I didn't know what was going on. I came to in the town centre around 6 a.m. I'd just been walking about, I think, and decided to go to the red-light area. Speed makes you horny. There was this hooker, and she took me round the back of an old pub. She wanted the money and I had none.'

'Right.'

'How long do you think I'll get for that?'

'What did you do?'

'I fucked her anyway, and didn't pay her.'

'I take it she wasn't happy with that arrangement.'

'No, she struggled for a bit but soon stopped. She's a whore, man. That's what they do. She probably enjoyed it.'

He started snivelling again. I let him carry on.

'How long do you think I'll get?'

I'd heard so many of these stories that I knew what troubled him. His tears weren't shed for the victim, they were cries for his change in circumstances. I wouldn't sugar-coat it for a scumbag like Kilkenny.

'The starting point for rape is five years.'

I could see him doing the maths: five years, out in two and a half. He'd done over four years for his previous offence so less than that wouldn't bother him. I gave him a few moments of peace.

'Although that depends on the aggravating factors. If there was violence, that would be frowned upon. Use of drugs and alcohol would be another negative aspect, so you would likely be looking at eight years. I guess if you got a superb brief, he could argue that you thought it was a business arrangement. Say she was a hooker and you wanted to pretend it was rough. Maybe you forgot you had to pay.'

He liked that, fool that he was.

'Unfortunately, you have a conviction for a previous sexual offence.'

His eyes narrowed as he tried to think how I would know.

'A serious one, if I'm not mistaken. That would make you a dangerous man. Are you a dangerous man, Mr Kilkenny?'

The idiot had the incredible pride to puff his chest out.

'I'll say.'

'I thought as much. When you go to court, you will receive a life sentence.'

'What?'

'Life, probably with a minimum term of fifteen years. You won't get out after fifteen years though, as they will say you're still a danger. You would need to keep your nose clean and, even then, I would be surprised if you were out in twenty. How old are you now?'

He sat down on the bed. No tears this time. They would come.

'Thirty.'

'You'll be fifty when you leave. About the same age as me.'

I stood up and pressed the intercom. A muffled indecipherable buzz came through.

'Listener, guv. Ready to go.'

I turned to stare at Kilkenny. There would be no more talking from him for a while. I wanted to get out of there fast, though. A man like him would look for someone else to blame.

* * *

In some ways watching the beatings was worse as, even though Kilkenny wasn't as bulky any more, his anger had developed.

When people like him were released they didn't nip down to their local Virgin Active and take out full membership, they picked up the reins of their old lives and rode hell for leather to their next mistake. He would have plenty of free time to rectify his muscle wastage, but he was still too strong for everyone on that wing.

There were Kilkennys in every jail and no governor wanted another one, so him leaving any time soon was unlikely. Occasionally they would do one-for-one swaps. You take our arsehole and we'll have yours. The fact that Kilkenny was still on remand meant there was no chance of him being transferred.

He did get caught for his violent ways and on the odd occasion went to the block. The problem was they could only send him back to one place: the VP wing. Kilkenny would then decide who was responsible for his plight and they would suffer.

The only person he left alone was my good self. I wasn't sure why. The other cons looked to me for guidance and help. I was an experienced man with many a story. There was a cachet to being a listener too. Perhaps it was because I had seen him at his most vulnerable.

I remembered Doc's words: 'Better someone else than us.' Back then, I'd thought they would come to haunt me. I was wrong – it was Doc who would have his own personal poltergeist.

What kind of person hurt a dying man? That was what happened though. It was as if Kilkenny blamed Doc for him being back. Doc wouldn't grass, no one ever saw anything, and he carried on refusing to go to the healthcare ward. I helped when I could, gave him my food, or got his for him when he couldn't get out of bed.

I was the only friend he had. He was also the only man I'd ever really spoken to since I'd been inside. He'd helped me when I first arrived and his presence helped now too, despite the unbearable conditions he was under. Things actually became worse as a new officer started on the unit. Even the other members of staff called him Treacle. He depended on Kilkenny to maintain control.

It was Treacle who told me my brother wanted to speak to me. I walked towards the office door, assuming he was on the phone. Treacle shot me a look of confusion.

'What are you doing?'

'Waiting to speak to my brother.'

'He's there. At the gate.'

Sure enough, my gaze followed his arm and there was Frank at the gates. Even though he was in normal clothing, and the bars were high, I still thought he looked diminished. I hadn't seen him for over a year. It must have been a tough twelve months.

'Frank. What's going on?'

'It's a long story, Vinnie. One we both played a part in.'

'Step away from the gate, please.'

The most wretched of souls could tell Treacle was weak-minded. My brother didn't even bother to respond to him. Treacle sneaked off to the office and left us alone.

'What happened?'

'You were aware I'd been having problems with the missus. Well, we had a few big drunken rows. I decided to leave. You know I've been there before, so I could see how it'd finish. I gave notice on my flat and when it was empty, I just moved back in there. That bitch reported me to the police. Told them I'd hit her.'

It was a strange moment. I believed him but it would be wrong to say there was no doubt in my mind.

'Vinnie, I didn't do it.'

Those were the words I'd chanted all those years ago. No one had believed me; I suspected they might not trust him either.

'I trust you, Frank. It must have been pretty bad for them to put you in jail.'

'That was the thing. The case didn't get to court, but they still took my DNA. It's been matched in connection with a murder.'

My mind scrambled through the past, looking for deaths. Was it natural to wonder who we knew that died and could Frank have been the one to kill them? If my belief in him was pure, I would have just told him not to worry and we'd get him through this.

Kilkenny arrived at the wing gate, returning from a visit with his girlfriend. I knew that because he had been shouting about it for weeks. Doc was coming back from one of his many healthcare appointments at the same time. They both stood next to us. Kilkenny looked witheringly at Doc.

'You still alive, you old pervert.'

He kicked Doc's walking stick away so he had to hang onto the bars for support.

'Do the world a favour and check out.'

Kilkenny's smile widened as he saw the family resemblance between Frank and me.

'Oh, lovely. Brother, is it? It will be fun for you to catch up. Perhaps you two sick fucks can get a pad together. I hear incest is beautiful.'

With the arrogance of someone who was top dog, he put his face millimetres from mine. 'Pathetic.'

As the smell of strong coffee and recently eaten chocolate left my face and swaggered down the wing, I caught the look of horror on Frank's face. He thought me pitiful, too.

'Who was that?'

'He's a prick, but he's too strong for us to do anything about it,' Doc answered.

Frank watched Kilkenny knock all the pool balls around the table to ruin the game that was being played as he walked past.

'He's one bloke. Use five of you, ten of you. Teach him a lesson.'

The arrival of a massive man distracted us. Frank felt the presence and turned around. His eyeline was level with the name badge of Senior Officer Cave.

'Are you on this wing?'

'No. I'm just talking to—'

The man didn't wait for an answer. He put a huge hand on Frank's arm and shoved him so violently that Frank had to run to stop himself falling over. Doc and I backed away from the gate.

'You know the rules. No talking at the wing gates.'

Cave walked off, steering Frank away like a farmer with a recalcitrant sheep. I went back to my cell to ponder Frank's arrest. Doc went back to his cell to consider Frank's revenge.

47

Doc shuffled into my cell first thing the next morning like an old, old man. His helper assisted him, a spry fellow we called Joe Sparrow. The prison often used other inmates to help some of the infirm to get dressed each morning, and generally assist. I wouldn't have thought they would have had Doc's plan in mind.

Doc's gasps echoed in the enclosed space, however, his eyes pierced the gloom.

'Would you be our lookout?'

'For what?'

'Kilkenny. Actually, kill Kilkenny.'

I didn't need to ask if it was a joke. He had the squared jaw of a man on a certain path. I also didn't need to ask why. A more worthless excuse for humanity I had yet to meet, and I had met them all.

It had been a rough night. I could count on few friends and, when things looked bad, it was a future with my brother that kept me going. The thought of him not being there when I got out was devastating.

I also realised that, even though I considered us close, there were huge gaps where I had no idea where he'd lived and what he'd been up to. He could literally have done anything. I still couldn't see Frank as someone capable of murder. He had a strong sense of right and wrong, on his own terms, but he knew taking a life was never the answer. I told Doc the same.

'You're not a killer, Doc.'

'No, but I know men who are.'

'I don't agree with taking someone's life, for whatever reason.'

'He will make my last few months here unbearable.'

'He hasn't done anything to me.'

'I knew you'd say that. That's why I wanted you to just be a lookout.'

'How are you going to do it? You can barely hold that walking stick, never mind take down a man that size.'

'I seen it done,' said Joe, on the balls of his feet.

'Numbers, we've got. He's made our lives a misery and there's plenty who would like some payback. His latest crime is going to get him a life sentence so he will be here forever. We'll never escape from him, and he will be free to bully us endlessly and relentlessly. Unless we take him.

'We'll get Kilkenny when he's in the shower. He goes every Sunday morning when most people are on the exercise yard or still in bed. We'll wait until Treacle is on duty and distract him in one of the cells. You know how he likes to look at the naked pictures some of the girlfriends send in.

'He never supervises exercise so the other officer will be out the way. It'll be just us and Kilkenny. We'll throw on body after body until he's as vulnerable as we've been. Then he'll understand how helpless and wretched we've felt under his unforgiving rule. I will deal the killing blow.'

'What you going to do, cut his jugular?'

I was being flippant. Doc smiled.

'Good guess, but that wouldn't work. I'm a doctor, remember. The jugular is for the movies. It's a vein. The carotid, on the other hand, is the artery that supplies blood to the brain. That's the one you need for a quick job.

'Actually, we have two carotid arteries and two vertebral arteries responsible for brain oxygenation. There is also a polygon of collateral circulation that provides blood to the brain if one of the arteries is lost.'

He beamed at me. Weird how the mind works. I supposed that must have been some kind of stored memory from when he was at medical school. Fascinating, obviously, but a little unnecessary for the current audience.

'The carotid, then.'

'Yes, both if possible, but it's not as easy as you may think. They are inside the neck amongst other tissue. If we make a mistake and don't incapacitate him, he will kill us instead.'

A cornered and wounded Kilkenny was a worrying prospect.

'How long would it take if we severed one of his carotids?'

'Around eight to ten seconds at a guess. As you can imagine, there haven't been any studies to assess the rate of loss of consciousness. He would definitely bleed out in a few minutes and there's no way they would have the expertise on hand to save him. It'll be messy and I don't suppose he'll just let us do it.'

Never had a truer word been spoken. It was ridiculous to be discussing the facts as though we were about to perform a life-saving operation. The stakes, in some ways, were higher.

'You'll be murderers. All of you, even those that stand watch.'

'It'll never come to that. I'll stay with the body and confess to the murder. We're going to make a weapon in the woodwork class. I'll tell them I surprised him and then finished him off. There are no cameras in the showers, and the one that's near the office, we'll smudge with toothpaste. Nobody else knows anything. I'll be long dead before it ever goes to trial.'

'Got it all worked out. Who's going to help? Karen?'

Karen was the heroin addict I'd met seven years past. Turned out his nickname was actually Charon, (pronounced Ka-ron) after the mythical Greek ferryman who carried the souls of the newly deceased across the River Styx and into the Underworld. He was usually depicted as a living skeleton in a cowl so it was a witty comparison. Unfortunately, he'd been in prison so many times over the years it had evolved into Karen.

Charon himself would have been a handier assistant.

'Yes, Karen, Bomber, Deadly Leadley and Johnno. Joe Sparrow and Rolt as distraction.'

They weren't a hopeless crew for a desperate job. Karen had long given up on life and would be easily swayed by the weakest of rewards. A few bags of brown would do the trick. Bomber was a big black man called Cedric Boumba from somewhere in Africa. He was a rapist.

Johnno was in for murder. He was still on trial, so innocent until proven guilty and all that. If you believed his story, there were extenuating circumstances, but he'd still slain his own parents. Morally, he should have been on the wrong side of every argument. Maybe he had a taste for murder now.

Deadly Leadley was his prize asset. He came from Poland and was in for a long stretch. He'd done some terrible things to a woman he'd kept in a shed, and had been told it was unlikely he would ever be released. He was aggressive and had little to lose. Ironically, he had received his nickname for being a bully. Apart from Karen and Joe, they were young strong men. They would have a chance.

Doc's posse was a foul collection of God's mistakes. It wasn't right that they were judge and jury, Kilkenny the accused, and

Doc the executioner. I'd always said normal rules didn't apply, but perhaps they did? They did say you would be judged by a jury of your peers so maybe it was apt. I didn't want any part of it.

I walked to the telephones at the back of the wing and telephoned Silent Kevin. It rang out, but I stayed and looked down at the inmates. I could see Bomber and Leadley playing pool together and laughing. Prison was a strange place. They were unhappy about being bullied, yet I suspected if they had the chance to rule the wing themselves, they would do. Their deeds were as bad if not worse than Kilkenny's.

Prisons should run self-awareness courses. Drum it into them that there isn't a hierarchy of crimes, even though the sentencing makes it seem that way. There is no such thing as a victimless crime.

If Kilkenny had given up the right to be treated as a human being, then so had most people in these places. Nevertheless, he would still have a mother, siblings, children, or innocent others whose lives would be shattered by the taking of his life.

Those who have nothing to lose are the most dangerous in any society. How can you beat the suicide bomber when he is prepared to sacrifice everything?

Doc was a dead man walking. He was so close to the end that you could sense death's hand on his shoulder. However, revenge is a powerful motivator. Maybe the strongest of urges. That was all he had left. It would give him the energy to commit one last heinous act.

48

I hadn't slept all night. Treacle was on first thing in the morning with another new officer and the beating was planned. That was right. I'd persuaded them it would be better to teach him a lesson than commit that most final of crimes. They were concerned that if it didn't go well, he would hunt them down, one by one, and they'd never escape from his violent reign.

However, they agreed, albeit reluctantly, that they would become worse people than Kilkenny if they went through with a murder.

My role was simple. I had to stand at the entrance to the showers and warn them if anyone came. Now it was set to go ahead, the planning of it seemed complicated. There were too many variables: he might alter his routine, or the phone could ring, or anything in fact. It wasn't like we could change the plan and delay as Doc was fading fast. Without his leadership, the task would fail.

I paced up and down in the cell. Did sit-ups, star jumps, press-ups, anything to distract my mind. That was one of the worst things about prison: the lack of being able to go for a walk. I suspect it's what drives captive animals wild.

The act of stretching your muscles, filling your lungs, and leaving your cares and all others behind you, at least for a while, is many a thing's salvation. The tiger in his cage paces up and down, up and down, going madder and getting angrier by the stride. No wonder they maul people when they get the chance.

Nothing could distract me, and I gave in and focused on what would soon occur. I believed life would be different afterwards. I knew something would go wrong, almost as if I could feel the atmosphere in the air was charged differently.

The digital clock on the TV became my focus, and I watched the minutes tick by. More life lost. Sometimes in the past I'd stared at the time on the microwave as it heated my soup and thought watching the seconds count down was a waste. I used to make myself wipe a surface or tidy a cupboard instead. However, inside my time had no value, so I threw it away.

Eventually my door opened and I unclenched my fists. I stepped out of my cell and watched Treacle, and the other unlucky soul whose life would also be damaged that day, unlock the top landing. Bomber and Leadley came out of neighbouring cells and nodded at each other. I watched them turn and stare down to the final cell on their floor and wait for Doc to appear. Their faces gradually built worried expressions.

Just as Bomber moved to go down there, Doc appeared. He shuffled out of his cell, hunched over, like Yoda when he was at the end. He rested his walking stick on the railing. That was the sign. It would happen today.

If sex offenders are in a jail with regular inmates, they exercise at different times. Otherwise they would get abuse, and possibly tarmac or some other projectile, thrown at them from the other yards. As usual, at five to eleven came the call. 'Exercise to the gate.'

It was a warm morning, the kind that reminded you of where you were and what other people might be enjoying. Despite that, few would resist the chance for some warmth and natural light.

The wing occupants sensed trouble that day and everyone who wasn't involved left the wing. Treacle closed the gate behind the last person and returned to his office. He then started something we called 'bolts and bars', and the prison called AFCs – Accommodation Fabric Checks.

Each morning, one officer had to go to every cell and check the fixtures and fittings hadn't been loosened for weapons or escape purposes. They also checked for bottles of hooch or any other unauthorised items. There were fifty-six cells on our wing, so it would take him over an hour. Exercise was an hour. All we needed now was Kilkenny to do what he always did: take a shower.

I played table tennis with a weak-chinned lad, Rolt, who had received eighteen months for amassing the biggest collection of child porn in Suffolk for many a year. I actually found Rolt more objectionable than every other person on the wing.

He'd tried to tell me, when he first arrived, that he hadn't touched any children, so what did it really matter? It wasn't like he'd taken the pictures. The stuff was on the Internet for anyone to look at, so what difference did it make? I think I would have been incensed if I hadn't been so shocked.

I explained that, by watching those pictures and movies, he created a demand for them. Two crimes were being committed. A child was abused to make the pictures, and he committed a crime by watching. If many viewed them, more would be made, and further children would suffer. He looked at me in the same way you would if someone quoted you forty pounds for a burger.

I often wondered at the strange nature of some of the sickest minds in Britain playing table tennis with each other. Maybe the monotonous ping and pong was a tranquilliser for our troubled minds. Actually, not mine. As always, when I played table tennis with Rolt, I imagined beating him to death with the bat. It made it more enjoyable, made me expend more effort, and was surprisingly tiring.

Neither of us put our backs into it that day as we both had roles to play. Leadley and Bomber were playing pool badly, trying not to watch Treacle walk in and out of each cell. I saw Johnno poke his head out of the showers, wondering what the delay was. Doc and Karen talked on the phones, possibly to each other, but of the main man, there was no sign.

Treacle finished the lower landing and skipped up the stairs. Kilkenny came out of his cell with a towel round his bare shoulders. It was against the rules to be on the wing without a shirt on, yet Treacle didn't give him a second glance and ducked into the first cell to avoid confrontation.

Kilkenny strutted down the steps as if he were Sinatra coming on stage. My hackles rose. They were flattened by the incredible definition of Kilkenny's chest. I hadn't thought he was as big as last time I saw him, but perhaps that was fat. Power and fluidity shone from him and I felt afraid. We would need more men.

Kilkenny's presence froze Rolt with fear. I hammered the ball at him but only Rolt's eyes followed as it fired past and towards Kilkenny's face. I took a step back. He caught the ball and suspended it in the air between two fingers. It was at his mercy, as were we, waiting to be crushed.

After what seemed like hours, yet could only have been seconds, he bounced it off the back of Rolt's head and swaggered away. Doc and Karen came over from the phones. When they got to the last cell before the office, Doc knocked five times on the door. The small old man, Joe Sparrow, popped out and followed the rest to the showers.

I couldn't help but think of Captain Ahab as Doc beckoned me to follow. The final person to go in, apart from Doc, was Karen. He dragged a sock from his pocket and dropped in two pool balls. He felt its heft and twisted it round his hand.

My position as lookout meant I could see in the showers and down the landing at the same time. Upstairs, I saw Rolt going towards the last cell Treacle had visited. The distraction was in place, so we were clear to proceed. What I saw in the showers, though, beggared belief.

Johnno lay unconscious in one of the corners. Kilkenny grappled with Bomber, while Leadley tried to pull him over by the legs. He would have had similar success pulling two pine trees over. Bomber slipped on the wet floor and Kilkenny drove a huge haymaker onto the top of his head. He slumped.

Leadley was losing his grip, meanwhile Karen was swinging his improvised mace around with wild abandon. Joe Sparrow had a sharpened pool cue in his hand and jabbed away at Kilkenny as effectively as a lion tamer with a broom. Joe was rightfully more concerned by being hit by Karen. Kilkenny grabbed the sock as it flew past and yanked. Surprisingly, Karen didn't let go and barged into him, causing them to stagger back and trip over Bomber. They all rolled on the floor.

'Do something,' Doc whispered.

Oddly, it was quiet. The occasional grunt of effort but no energy was wasted in shouting. The scene reminded me of the late Steve Irwin and his crew trying to suppress an enormous crocodile as it lashed out. This croc was winning.

All that kept Kilkenny on the floor was the old man jabbing at his face and Karen, who wriggled like an electric current was going through him. Bomber and Leadley were done.

I'd seen it regularly with violence inside. Too often, the bulk was manufactured with steroids, which would give at the first challenge. Even if the hard yards had been spent in the gym, they were of limited use. Enormous muscles on big men used massive amounts of energy so after impressive demonstrations they were a spent force.

The wiry types kept fighting. Kilkenny was in control. He began to wind me up. All through this potentially deadly assault, his face hadn't changed. A small grin shone, as if he had expected it, and cared little. He finally got an arm around Karen's neck and subdued him.

'Please, Vinnie. He'll win. Think of what he did to that innocent girl.'

'What girl? The prostitute?'

He gave me a strange look.

'It wasn't a prostitute. She was a checkout girl. On her way to work for the 7 a.m. shift at Tesco, she used a shortcut through the park. Kilkenny waited in the bushes. He dragged her in and raped her whilst holding a broken bottle to her neck to keep her quiet. He took ages. It was the drugs, he couldn't finish.'

The mist came down like a lightning flash. I strode towards the now sitting Kilkenny and grabbed the pool cue out of the old man's hand. I powered into Kilkenny and pushed his back to the floor, trapping his free arm with my knee. I knew fear, and then so did he.

The sharpened tip pressed against his neck and I tensed my muscles as Kilkenny's eyes bulged in anticipation. Then, nothing. I didn't want to kill anyone, whatever they'd done. I relaxed my grip. The only sounds were the heavy breathing of tired men. A small smell of illness and an exhausted pant approached my side.

Doc knelt down with a cough, put two hands on top of the cue and drove it through Kilkenny's neck until it hit the solid floor. He took a tea towel out of his belt and wiped the pool cue. He stared at me with the same smile that Kilkenny had worn. I looked down at Kilkenny's stunned face as the blood collected around his collar.

Karen struggled free, pulled Bomber and then Leadley to their feet, and left. I turned and watched the old man slip away. Johnno was gone too. The metallic smell assaulted my nostrils and I backed up. I supposed Kilkenny could have moved but maybe he understood the moment the cue retracted, his life would pour from his body in seconds. It was a strange sight. Doc might have been saving him in another lifetime.

'I knew you'd do that, Vinnie. We couldn't have done it without you. I'm sorry for lying to you about only hurting him. The world will be a better place.'

Doc gasped and put a hand to his heart and I stepped towards him.

'A screw is coming,' came the shout.

'Go. Leave now.' He tried to take a huge breath but failed. I was walking away as I heard his final whispered piece of advice. 'It's almost funny,' he managed. 'You're frightened of life, and we're scared of you. Let the creature out, Vinnie. It's who you really are.'

I moved to the exit and took a final look. My friend, Doc, had cheated me with his dying breaths. He pulled the cue out and blood flowed into the drains. Kilkenny's arms came up and held Doc's wrists as one of his legs twitched. Doc leaned back and drove his weapon into Kilkenny's eye socket.

As I staggered down the wing, I realised I knew Doc about as well as I knew myself. He was sick and bad, and I hadn't seen it. But there lurked something uncontrollable inside me and he'd known it. I was no better than him and he'd won. I'd become an accessory to murder. Another award to add to my role of honour on judgement day.

I sat on the small plastic seat in my cell and put my head in my hands. I searched my memory for those nights with Kirsty that had sent me to this place. The past blurred after so much time. The monotony and routine in here had consumed me. I had two more years to do, looking at the same screaming faces. What was the point?

An appointment slip on the floor of my cell caught my eye, which I hadn't noticed in my fervour to get out of sight. Visit hall, 3 p.m. in a week's time, with Frank Roach. I supposed they couldn't let him on our wing to talk, so he'd arranged it through the visit department. Thank God for that. I had heard nothing from him for a while.

The previous week he'd passed a message to the orderly saying they'd moved him to the remand wing, and that he would get an appointment for us to discuss our case. 'Our case' – those were the words he'd used. I tried, again, to recall what he meant by them. Still, I could feel myself sinking. At least a chat with him was something to look forward to.

Too soon we forget the horror of what we've done. People had died and I'd taken a hand, and yet there I was thinking normally. I would need to keep my calm. Sweat beaded on my forehead as I thought of the amount of men on whose silence we now relied. If one broke, we would all go down.

The noise on the wing elevated. Even in my cell, I heard a multitude of heavy footwear running towards the showers. Muffled swear words and barked orders echoed around the ceiling. I turned my TV on and raised the volume. No doubt they would come for me soon.

49

We hugged when we got to the visit hall. Frank's bones jarred my arms. I held his shoulders afterwards and looked from eye to eye.

'You okay?'

'I'm coping, just. I don't know how you've put up with this for so long.'

'When you get given as much time as I did, it's better than the other option.'

We sat down. An officer kindly came over and gave us a cup of coffee each as inmates weren't allowed to go to the little shop. It felt like a normal visit except neither of us would go home.

'I guess you need to do some talking, Frank. What happened?'

He took a deep breath and my life went full circle.

'I'm sure you remember our night out in Cromer when we drove there to see if we could find that French girl, Sara. Three boys attacked us. After our fight, one of them died, and one of them hovered in a coma for months. He wasn't the same afterwards, which only left a single witness.

'He told the police a gang of men attacked them, five or something. That we beat the shit out of them, smashed a man to pulp on a post and repeatedly kicked another in the head. His bruised and battered body confirmed his story.

'Afterwards, when he sobered up, he couldn't picture our faces, or recall many details. Not surprising, seeing as there were only two of us. They had no evidence, no witnesses, no weapons, nothing. All they had was my blood at the scene, which didn't match anything on their database.

'It was a dark night and long before CCTV. After they arrested me for that assault, they took my DNA. It was cross-checked at some point and matched and here I am. Charged with murder and manslaughter as the second one died six years ago.'

He sat back in his seat and it was his turn to eyeball me. My mind wandered from how unfair life could be when we were the victims, to the terrifying realisation of what he'd said. I'd killed a man by bashing him against a post. The one I'd kicked died too. Years later, but undeniably due to my actions.

'Shit.'

'Quite. Hard to believe that something so long ago would come along and bite us in the arse.'

'What did you say when they arrested you?'

'Nothing, I said nothing. I remember the stitch-up that you went through.'

'What will you say? When you go to court?'

'I'll tell them what happened. Three men chased me and a friend of mine. They attacked and we fought them off. That's it. We left, not knowing they were injured as we feared for our lives. If they find the bouncers who chucked us out, they'll confirm that we were only two. I missed off the part about you goading them in the nightclub.'

'Goading who? What do you mean? Everyone was staring at us.'

'You had that look on your face, Vinnie. The one that scares people, and you were scanning the room like Robocop. It's not entirely surprising they had the hump.'

'You started it by elbowing that bloke under the chin in the club.'

'He told me they were going to kill you. His exact words.'

'It didn't necessarily mean they would.'

'Look, they chased us and we defended ourselves. Don't worry, I haven't mentioned I was with you. I know I'm partly responsible for what happened. When they asked who the other person with me was, I named an old navy friend, one who's now long dead.'

'Thank you.'

I let the consequences of our actions filter through my brain. Absorbing what was important and discarding the rest.

'You could go down for murder.'

'It's his word against mine. I just have to hope he will cave under questioning.'

'Bloody hell. Why not tell them the truth? We did what had to be done.'

That phrase came out unintentionally and my brother finally lost his temper.

'Vinnie. Listen to yourself. You did what had to be done? You killed a man. That's Mum talking and she was insane. You aren't God. Life's not like that. Can't you see Mum for what she was?'

I considered his words. We used to joke that she was crazy. Perhaps it wasn't so funny. The phrase that arose in my mind like a ghostly apparition was one my mother often said: 'In the end, the only judgement that matters is that of your children'. That was a strange thing to say. Taking into account what we now knew about her, we'd have to be mad ourselves to condone her behaviour.

However, I didn't have children, so maybe I didn't understand.

Did a mother's love and protection outweigh any other considerations? There seemed to be nothing she wouldn't do to protect her family. History was full of people lying to save their offspring. Not killing, though. I couldn't condone that kind of thinking.

We pretended to be civilised, but so many were consumed and controlled by animalistic drives that proved otherwise. My mum's statement confirmed that. Only someone psychotic would make such an absolute declaration.

'Are you saying our mum was a psychopath?'

'Do you know what, I researched it. Psychopaths view their innocent victims as inhuman objects. That fits her a little. Although, they are often smartly dressed, charming yet unemotional, and can also be intelligent. Does that sound like Mum?'

Strange how he'd looked it up too. I thought of my mum in her baggy jeans from the charity shop, slopping cider on her top as she laughed her head off at my dad's terrible jokes.

'No, not quite. Pretty far from it, in fact. So, what was she?'

'I checked out sociopaths too. They at least have a conscience, but it's flimsy. They may know stealing or killing is wrong, and might feel guilt or remorse, but that wouldn't stop them doing it. It sounds closer, but I think she was just unstable, or easily scared and prone to lashing out. Perhaps she inherited a terrible murderous temper. One she passed down the line?'

What was he implying?

'Why, Frank? Is that you? Do you feel insane? Do you have the urge to kill?'

'Not me, Vinnie. You.'

My eyes widened to protest and I felt a shiver go through my body. Frank's words put me in a box; he closed the lid and hammered it shut with facts. Nail after nail. Some facts vivid, others remembered. All familiar.

50

'The boy up the slide. That was you. I tried to get you to let him down, but you were like a demon. Dad called you his "Devil child", but it was only half a joke. Your destructive rages would come from nowhere and sweep through the house. Hurting people, physically and mentally, and breaking furniture and toys with any part of your body available.

'The reason you remember the cupboard under the stairs is because that's where our parents used to lock you. It was the only thing that calmed you down. You would sit in the dark on the little boxer's stool they put in there, and go quiet. When they opened the door an hour or so later, out you came as though nothing had happened.

'They didn't know what to do with you. We had experts come to the house and you had tests at the hospital. I wonder now if they knew of our mum's back story. They looked on in horror when they saw you torturing our toys and dolls.

'The day before your seventh birthday, you went in the road and a car hit you head-on. The driver was a debt collector who'd been hassling one of our neighbours. He swore you ran at his car and attacked him. We didn't say anything, and the police thought he was in shock. Clearly, we weren't surprised and could believe it. They induced a coma for a few days as you had a swelling on the brain. They told us we might lose you.'

'Mum told me I was chasing a dog when I had the accident.'

'I know. She thought it was for the best, because when you eventually came home, you'd changed. The past had been erased. You seemed to be able to pick up eating and talking, but we had to teach you to read and write again. You rarely read before, but afterwards it was all you wanted to do. It was as if you were desperately trying to find the information that could fill the holes in your memory.

'The violent outbursts stopped and loads of things scared you. I suppose they would have done because you hadn't seen them before. Like a child that's frightened by a dog or a clown because they haven't been close to one yet. Even adults are wary of new experiences as they don't know what to expect.

'It was kind of funny as we were nervous. If you tripped over or made a mistake, we held our breaths, waiting for you to explode. You didn't though. When kids bullied you at school, you looked at them like you couldn't understand what was going on.

'The one time you lashed out at them was when you stamped on John Victory's foot in the tuck shop queue. Mum went loopy when she found out. She blamed him and thought the beast was returning. I suppose that's why she did what she did.'

'I don't remember doing that. Are you sure?'

'Someone who was there told me. They said your face became blank and you stepped back and drove your heel into his. Afterwards, you stood there and smiled, as if nothing had occurred.'

'All this time, I thought you were the wayward son,' I said. 'The fighter. Always out and up to no good. I never went anywhere.'

'Mum and Dad cut me some slack if I looked after you. The amount of fights I got in protecting you was ridiculous. You were oblivious to what was happening. You didn't have any friends as you couldn't remember making any, or even understand how to be one. You became nervous of going out on your own because you had lost the confidence that familiarity provides.

'Underneath it all, though, you were a fantastic person. Brilliant with looking after Dad and helping out. You wanted nothing for yourself. I was confused after our parents died because I felt as if I'd let Mum down. That she had to kill Dad, so we wouldn't feel too guilty. How nuts is that?

'She recognised you in herself, Vinnie. She worried you would end up in prison like she did. I think she thought if you got cross, violence would return. That's why she instructed me to protect you, to stop people from provoking you.

'Until that point, I was normal, but not after she asked that. I loved football and just being a kid. Did you know I used to be in the top sets, and that I kept goal for the school team? I had to become something I'm not.

'The only person I'd had a fight with before that was you. Because you cut the limbs off my favourite Action Man. Even after that, you attacked me because I complained. Jesus, having to defend myself from my bonkers little brother. The fact she told me to be your shadow, and explained why, hung between us for the rest of her life. She regretted it but felt there was no other option. Maybe there wasn't.'

'What a family,' was all I could come up with.

'I said that to you before. Maybe there's something twisted in our DNA. It's why I never had children and was secretly relieved when you didn't. Whatever raged in you as a child is still there. The older you are, the stronger it becomes. You would have killed that bloke on your stag night if Kevin hadn't pulled you away.'

I immediately believed he was right. I had lost control. Desperate not to recall that evening, I changed the subject.

'Why don't you tell them the truth? That it was you and me who had that fight in Cromer.'

'I had a think about it. You've been through too much. Let me take this burden from you as I'm also to blame. It will make up for the time I disappeared too. Remember, twenty years ago, after I missed your wedding, I said I would make it up to you. This is me doing that, Vinnie.'

Then he nodded and smiled. What was I missing? Could it be guilt for all those lost years? I was sure he felt awful for not attending my wedding. Then it came and it was obvious. No wonder he didn't say it out loud.

'You have more chance of them believing you by saying you were with a dead guy, don't you? You do run the risk of him accusing you of killing the others, but he shouldn't be able to as he was fighting you at the time. You're worried I might lose my temper in court, shout they deserved it or something equally condemning. You reckon your odds are improved without me.'

He looked away, so I knew I was close, but hadn't quite hit the bullseye.

'Ah, now I get it. You don't want to stand up in the dock next to a sex offender serving eighteen years. I know what people think. Guilty of that, he is capable of anything. Send him down, send them both down, guilty as charged, no trial needed.'

He looked at me and shrugged. A gesture that broke my heart. He spoke slowly.

'It's true though, isn't it? You are better off in here and away from it.'

We sat in silence, and I watched the other inmates kissing their wives and girlfriends. I saw drugs pass from one mouth to another. There were bored toddlers and terrified teenagers, unbelieving parents, and Frank and me. I didn't fit in this world. I'd now found out I never did. Frank whispered his latest news.

'They're moving me to Norwich prison tomorrow. It's why the director agreed to let us meet. The case will be heard at Norwich Crown Court, so I need to plead and then wait until it goes to trial. It might take a year.

'Unbelievable, isn't it? Due to the severity of the charges it's unlikely I'll get bail, so I'll have to stay inside all that time. I doubt they'll allow us to visit each other again, so this is goodbye, Vinnie. At least for a bit.'

I knew that was for the best, yet I felt pathetic because I couldn't help thinking he'd let me down. That he didn't trust me. The possibility of him going down for murder would leave me with only one friend. I said as much.

'Let's hope Silent Kevin doesn't move away, or I'll have nobody to ring.'

'Ah, I forgot about that.'

'Why? What happened?'

'Kevin is permanently silent. He was at his machine on the factory floor and went to see the nurse. Told them he felt short of breath. He sat on the bed they kept in there, said, "No" for some reason, lay down and died. A pulmonary embolism, they explained. Dead before his head hit the pillow.'

Kevin was gone too. Fury rose in me. It wasn't fair for one person to lose everything. My mind scrambled around for some normality, any kind of distraction.

'What's an embolism?'

'A big blood clot from the leg passed along his veins and blocked the flow in his lungs. He would probably have died in the hospital so he had no chance with the company first aider.'

I wasn't one of those prisoners who had found God, yet I still looked above, to ponder if things could get any worse. It didn't seem possible, but they would.

'Can I ask you a question, Vinnie? Be honest with me. You remember that bully, Kilkenny, the one who got stabbed to death in the showers on your wing? When he died, did you have anything to do with it?'

I'm not sure I'd ever lied to my brother, not so blatantly to his face. Maybe it was an impulsive response to him not trusting me.

'No, an old guy called Doc did it. They found him on top of Kilkenny holding the pool cue, while it was embedded inside his head. Doc was still alive at that point, and just before he passed out, he confessed. His last words were, "I do this for the world" – very melodramatic. He was dying anyway and never regained consciousness.'

I pondered over that afterwards; Doc and Kilkenny dying simultaneously. If there was an afterlife, it would be bad news for both. They would have been on the same elevator down. The hellevator, as Karen called it. That would certainly be poetic justice. Bonded in life and then screaming together in the Devil's house for ever more. Eternity with Kilkenny was a frightening prospect. That sounded like hell to me.

'How did he get the better of someone that big and strong?'

'No idea. He'd written a letter admitting his desire to "save the world from evil". They found it resting against the window in his cell. Included were fifty different times and dates when Kilkenny hurt or stole from him. He was gripping the murder weapon and provided his intentions and the motive.

'Funny how eighty men use those showers but nobody saw a thing. They asked around but never discovered any other explanation. I don't think they care too much though, and it's been quieter on there since he's gone. No one got into trouble apart from Treacle.'

'Who's he? The officer?'

I smiled. The prison grapevine was accurate, for once.

'Yes, we all get what we deserve in the end.'

'I heard that too. They found a load of stuff in Kilkenny's cell that had been brought into the jail for him – mobile phones, spice, gear. Bizarrely, even a receipt for the phone. It didn't take MI5 to trace that back, with Treacle's face clear on the CCTV and his fingerprints over everything. I wonder what Kilkenny had on him to get him to bring drugs and phones in for him.'

'I should think it was only fear. That would be enough.'

We contemplated those words and finished our drinks. An officer came by and gave us the nod. That was our time over. We shook hands, the earlier warmth lost somewhere in the last hour.

With Frank and Kevin gone, I would be alone. No one to miss me and nothing to wait for. I think I made my decision then, but it was a letter that killed me.

51

2016 – AGE: 50

Frank's lack of faith in me on that visit was a hurtful memory that stayed ever present. I struggled through Christmas but time had hung heavy. I gave up the listener job and trudged along to woodwork with the rest.

Although Kilkenny's absence left a vacancy, no one stepped up to fill it. People were wary of me again, as they had been at school. Prisoners still came with their problems and questions; however, they were reserved and respectful. On the odd occasion, I would catch someone pointing at me from across the landing.

When I looked in my blurred mirror, I felt like pointing at myself. I didn't recognise the man staring back. Even Frank saw me as somebody I never knew existed.

The officer that replaced Treacle was a happy lad. I often wondered how long he'd last. It was long enough for him to tell me I had a letter on my floor when I returned from work one afternoon.

Perhaps he was aware I got little post so thought it would cheer me up. Receiving any correspondence was an unusual event for me. Some cons constantly bothered the screws to see if they had any post. I'd never done that as I rarely received anything unless it was official, and I'd been away too many years for much of that.

It had been opened, of course, as they looked in all of our mail. Most of us weren't allowed any contact with children so everything was checked. This extended to pictures of kids, and, for the sickest, even ones of their own. They couldn't have read the letter I got that day or any sane person would have had me monitored.

The writing on the front was floral and made me think of a woman. The name that sprang to the forefront of my mind was Sara's. Maybe she had found me after all the years. I allowed myself a minute lying on my bed to recall that time. I remembered feeling the world was shrinking and as a person I was growing. Typical of my luck to end up in a prison.

Perhaps the staff only skimmed the first few lines and thought it a letter full of nostalgia, apologies and missed opportunities. They should have read on.

Dear Vinnie,

I decided to write to you to tell you I'm sorry. Actually, my therapist told me it might help. I've made a terrible mess of my life and fucked up a lot of innocent people. You paid the biggest price.

I bumped into Jake and Ben, the lads that I used to doss around with when I was young and lived near you. They saw you in our local prison. I'd heard you got such a long stretch. I couldn't believe it. I wondered at the time whether I should do anything about it, but I was out of control, so I didn't. I was already on the drugs, doing things to pay for them that make me ashamed. The stuff I put in my body helped me forget the sad life I'd lived.

I'm not sure this will help me or you, but I loved you, Vinnie. The awful stuff I so convincingly wrote about was done to me by that idiot boyfriend of my mum's. The one who froze to death.

My mum said to say that you did those terrible things. She knew you had won a load of money on the lottery and we'd get compensation. Otherwise, she said we were so skint that I would end up in foster care, where bad stuff happens – to young girls like me.

Obviously, she lied. We didn't get any money, or if we did, it didn't make any difference. I still ended up in care. Funnily enough, it was okay. My foster parents were nice but I missed my drunken mum.

I missed you too, Vinnie. I should have thought about it, but what could I do? It's only now I'm clean, sober, and older, that I realise how fucked up she was. Only now I understand how wrong we were.

I'm not sure if I'm asking for you to forgive me, or if I'm so horrible that I'm just trying to help myself. You didn't do those things to me. For a long time, you were all I had. Those nights you got in my bed were the only times I felt safe. I messed up, so bad, and you paid. Well, we all paid, and then some.

Some of the other things that have happened will be carried with me for the rest of my life. Don't think I haven't been punished. I have, many times, and in ways only a woman can be.

I don't know if this letter will help you in any way. Maybe you can get out early or something. I can't go to court though, or even leave an address. I'm in a refuge, the address is a secret, so I can't be exploited.

They tell me they can help me but I also need to help myself. Nights are bad. I still think of you, but I know I done wrong. I remember you saying how much you wanted your own children, well, I had mine, and lost them. It's been too long to get them back now, so I bring that with me too. More unwanted baggage that I can't set down.

There's a girl here, Alex, who was a teacher, said we need to start small. She helped me with this letter or there wouldn't have been any commas or apostrophes in it. I couldn't spell apostrophe either. She describes what we need to do as clinging to a few pieces from a jigsaw that's been cast into the wind.

A little arty farty if you ask me, I'm suspicious, but she says she's off the drugs. I understand the idea. We start again, build from the beginning. We may not find everything that's lost but we will have something pretty good at the end.

It's hard to think like that though. I want to be whole again, fresh and shiny. I'd love my teeth back too. Sorry, I'm rambling a bit.

The church people are coming over tonight. They mean well. They showed us knitting, which I'm pants at, and make us play strange games like Beetle. It's some messed-up shit. I have to pinch myself to let me know this is actually my life. I could kill a bottle of vodka when the singing starts.

It's weird, but I feel better after. Nice people with no agenda is what my therapist says I need. I reckon that's bull-shit, bet they feel dead pleased with themselves afterwards, helping us poor screw-ups. And fuck the therapist, she gets paid, or there's no way her ass would be here.

I've kind of lost my train of thought. I'm gonna send this anyway. Vinnie, I hope you are as well as can be expected. If my maths is right, you'll be out next year. Perhaps one day we'll meet for a beer.

Cheers, K

I let out the breath I'd been holding and slowly sat on my bed. I knew at the start it wasn't from Sara as she only called me Vincent. A letter from Kirsty was unexpected though. I placed it on the table as if any sudden movement might cause damage, and waited for the rancour that I now understood was part of me to burst to the surface.

Instead, there was nothing. Even the prison stilled. Almost as if it wanted me to concentrate on that moment. I gingerly picked up the paper and read again.

Afterwards, I cried and cried. For my life, I suppose, most of all, but also for my brother's. His was sent off course before he had any control. Who knows what might have happened if he had been left to be a child? I thought of my parents, their dreams, our victims, and shed a tear for everyone. For Kirsty, I wept, the greatest sorrow of them all.

What had my life been, and where was it going? Behind those bars, I just existed. Like Kirsty, I'd never be fresh and shiny again either. I tried, I know I did. I just failed.

52

I think that's what I was waiting for. I didn't want to go to my end thinking I had done wrong by her. Her letter released me. Some of my motivations, such as becoming a listener, had been an attempt to make sure someone, anyone, would know me as something other than forgotten vermin. That's probably how I will be remembered anyway, in the unlikely event they whisper my name.

Kirsty's acknowledgement of the facts as how I recalled them has stopped me thinking I misused my life. I spoke to Joe Sparrow about the letter. He said it meant nothing legally. I could have sent it myself. However, the pressure from the crushing weight of a life not lived was lifted from me. I had done right by Kirsty and that provided some solace. It made my choice a simple one.

To think, all these years, I was scared of life. The reality was that I was right to be afraid. Not of the world though, but of myself. Death and disaster followed my family around. We were an ocean liner steaming through life, the wash a turbulent mishmash of dead, imprisoned, and damaged bodies.

I knew what worked as I'd heard others tell me what they were going to do. I fashioned two wedges from some softer wood in the workshop. There was obviously no rope available but a hundred things work just as well.

I used a bedsheet, twisted into shape. I lent a few of my more precious items out to people on the wing who had little, knowing they would keep them afterwards. There was nobody to tell. Besides, it wasn't the time for a change of heart.

That night, I took a final wander around the landings. I passed a conversation where they were discussing the unfairness of our legal system. Innocent, of course, those moaning men were. 'Eight years, I've done,' I told them as I crept past. All I got were the pitiless frowns from uninterested and inconvenienced bystanders.

The same spirits who quietened the prison when I needed to think were absent when I wanted to die. They had lost control of the wing next to ours after they served the evening meal. The country mince had raw meat in it apparently. Or should that be allegedly? I thought mine tasted funny. Typical of us lot not to complain on the VP unit.

The hardened souls in mainstream were not so law abiding. A burning smell was in everyone's teeth. They locked our wing in a rush and didn't notice the loop of material I had left at the top of the door as it banged shut. They would need all of their staff to put out the fires and reclaim control from the bigger, angrier men. So, I waited.

A little over an hour later I heard the roar of protesters as the gates clanged open and the tornado squad charged. In those few minutes – it never took long for them to give in – I used my filled-up flask to hammer in the wedges. The loop hung down, so I tested the weight. It would do. After all, it only needed to hold for a bit.

What do you think of in those last few moments? I thought I would relive the bad things I'd done, yet I was wrong. They said your mother would always be in your thoughts.

I thought of mine. I recalled her sayings and remembered her sadness. What did she say? 'Why do people rush to their deaths? It is one appointment they'll never miss.' Nevertheless, in the end, she was early for hers too.

I remembered Frank and Kevin, and my dad's booming laugh. I imagined the funfair, hot bodies on cold sheets, dancing with Sara, and giggling with Clara. Maybe it's your soul, digging up the good things, to remind you there could be hope. Please don't give up.

I watched the news; it's not the real world. When I saw the politicians, enraged with false fury, and the doleful celebrities, gilded in wealth, I wondered if they knew of me, at the bottom of life. Will I be missed – does anyone care?

The shouts and the frenzy died down. It was time. The TV buzzed for a few seconds after I turned it off and then it was as peaceful as it was likely to be.

I placed the loop over my head with my back to the door and sat down. The sheet stretched with my weight but constricted with me poised six inches off the floor. That would be the difference between living and dying.

Gently, I departed. My eyes bulged and drooped. It felt like drowning. I tucked my hands in my pockets to stop them reaching for safety. The light faded and each piece of me went with it. As if the wind was blowing a pile of papers away.

At the end, it was rightfully just fear that remained. Fifty years of it. Then, as it was in life, we left together.

EPILOGUE

Prison Custody Officer Teresa Griffin walked into the hub where the senior officer controlled the wings. He was long gone, of course. The disturbance of the riot earlier had knackered her schedule, and she had a page of jobs like a menu.

She remembered being keen when they first offered her the role of IC. That meant 'In Charge', of a wing of sex offenders in her case. Awesome. It was called the safeguarding wing now. A strange turn of phrase for two landings of mostly sick-minded people. They had been sent to prison to protect the public. Yet here, they were taken out of main circulation for their own safety.

She'd given up looking on the computer to find out what they were in for. It didn't matter. She had a job to do and they were still human beings. However, it was gone 9 p.m. and she'd only just finished the paperwork. She should have left two hours ago. Although better to do it now than first thing in the morning.

The night staff worker was Operational Support Officer Mo Maher. She was setting up her snacks and reading material for the night. They got less money, but in some ways they had the best of it. At least everyone was locked up when they were here.

Mo was one of the good ones. She cared about the prisoners and did the job how it was supposed to be done.

'Here's the handover sheet, Teresa. Anything I should be aware of?' Mo said.

'Apart from the uprising earlier?'

They both smiled.

'Yes, I'm up to speed on that. Everyone's usually pretty quiet after the excitement. I've got three first night observation sheets and two ACCT books. Nothing on your wing, is there?'

ACCT stood for Assessment, Care in Custody and Teamwork. They were generally used for suicide and self-harm. Depending on the probability of something happening, inmates were observed up to five times an hour.

'No, that's it.'

'Okay, sweetie, have a good night. Wine o'clock for you.'

'Thanks, and you too, Mo. I hope they behave for you.'

Teresa stopped herself at the door.

'Actually, there might be something. Vincent Roach in cell twenty. He's not on an obs book or anything, but he seemed different today. Almost happy. It looked like he'd given some of his stuff away too.'

'No worries, I'll look in on him as well. I'm doing my rounds now.'

Mo waved to Teresa as she left and went to the induction wing. Nowadays, everyone who came in the prison underwent observations on their first night. It was prime time for self-harm and suicide. The cells were supposed to be suicide proof, but there were always ways.

A man had killed himself using his shoelaces as a tourniquet around his neck and tightening it with a small pencil. She struggled to imagine a more gruesome way to go. All three men waved back at her from the three cells she checked. She'd seen them all before on numerous occasions. Prison didn't hold many fears for the frequent flyers.

The two ACCT books were on the detox wing. Those two men had expressed dark feelings, so a book had been opened. Both said they had anxiety and depression. That was hardly unexpected.

If you regularly took drugs and got sent to prison where you were forced to go cold turkey, it wasn't surprising you felt anxious and depressed as a result. She decided to leave them until later. Then she could try to have a chat with them if they were still awake. That way, she could see what frame of mind they were in.

First, she would have a look in on Vincent Roach. She walked through the open wing gates and noted the safeguarding unit was quiet. To be fair, it often was.

She heard the main house block door open behind her and saw the officer who would run the prison tonight. Senior Officer Gardner waved and headed for the hub. Cheeky twat would eat all her biscuits if she wasn't quick.

She opened the observation panel on Roach's door and stared at an empty room. Panic coursed through her. Surely, he hadn't got out? The television was dormant and the bed made. Experience enabled her to calm herself. Even though the metal doors are locked, they rattle in the frame. She knew to nudge it with her knee to see if there was anything against it. There was a dead weight. She could see an outline of a body through the crack.

'Mr Roach, get away from the door. I need to see your face.'

There was no response.

'Vincent, move, now!' she shouted. Still no sound came from the cell.

Gardner came running to the wing.

'What's up?'

'Roach, sitting against the door. Non-responsive.'

They both knew what that meant.

Gardner ran back to the wing gates and locked them, in case it was a ruse. He spoke into his radio.

'QB, Gardner here. I'm breaking night state to open Charlie 20 on the safeguarding wing. Possible medical incident. Put the radio on call through. All available outstations to attend.'

'QB received. Romeo 1 and 2 en route. ETA ninety seconds.'

Gardner unlocked the door and had to push the body away to get it to open. Vincent Roach was blue and still. Mo already had her ligature knife out and cut the home-made noose. Gardner pulled the body out of the cell and knelt beside it.

'He's not breathing, I don't think he's breathing.'

'Vincent, wake up!' she yelled.

'QB, code blue. I repeat, this is a code blue. Charlie 1 wing. Medical staff to attend immediately. Attempted suicide.'

Mo put her fingers next to Vincent's larynx. Gardner hovered in position to begin CPR. They stared at each other as they paused. Seconds crept by. A slight gasp broke the silence.

'I've got a pulse.'

* * *

2017 – Present day

I survived. It was close for a while. However, I pulled through and spent long months in the prison healthcare unit. I wasn't grateful to start with and they disturbed me day and night with people peeking through my observation panel to make sure I wasn't looking for a way out. Finally, I got the help I needed and decided I wanted to live.

Prison inreach identifies and treats prisoners with mental disorders. I was classified as such and, with still over a year to go,

I had time to take advantage of the support they offered. No end of professionals saw me and I took part in courses and studies. To them, I was still an unrepentant, convicted sex offender but the other parts of my behaviour were examined.

There are some who believe the temperamental traits that lead to sociopathy and psychopathy are genetic. A child of someone with the condition may inherit a predisposition for the disorder.

There are also those who think parenting, specifically nurturing, and their general environment, can prevent an antisocial personality before it fully develops. Therefore, I can probably thank my mother twice for my madness.

We, as humans, always want to label things. It helps us understand the world but rarely is life that simple. My unusual behaviour as a young boy could have just been that: I was a bad kid. Anyone with children knows someone with a child who is incredibly naughty. Maybe it's you who is reading this, you're the one who has the lad nobody wants to call wicked. We don't name them as such, as nearly all of these children grow up to be perfectly normal adults.

There are some misbehaving kids who are able to control themselves, perhaps wait their turn, if the incentive is big enough. Others simply can't moderate their behaviour. There are no blood tests for conditions such as ADHD, and there was little understanding back when I was a boy.

Surprisingly, what they found more damaging was my loss of memory after the accident. I grew up not really knowing who I was. Understandably, my mother didn't want to remind me of my previous conduct.

I learnt all I thought I needed to know through books and the little narrative my parents and brother provided. It's no wonder I didn't turn out to be a rounded individual. Perhaps my murderous rages were just frustration. I had limited experience of dealing with provocation, hostility and aggression. Maybe it was only natural for me to respond with the normal animal urges we are born with. We fight, or we flee.

I discussed the incidents I had in my youth. For a few months, we even had a psychiatrist on the wing. As I said before, there are no barriers to entry for paedophilia. He was more interested in the fact that I'd had the chance to finish Kilkenny off and didn't. To him, that was a defining point in the examination of my personality. He thought that made me a good person. While under the most incredible tension, I had still not committed that dreadful act.

The other events, you could argue, were just growing up, and fights. I didn't set out to kill those boys who chased us that dark evening. I feared for my life and in self-defence most actions are, if not excusable, explainable.

We would never know if I would have killed that boy on my stag night but, again, it was something I hadn't started myself. How would you have reacted if someone was trying to stab your brother?

I wouldn't regard myself as normal, yet I don't consider myself a freak. In light of this, my suicidal tendencies decreased. As for what happened to Titch, the ex-boxer, well, I'm far from perfect.

The final brick on the path to recovery was that of Frank's release. A few weeks before the trial started, the boy who survived changed his story. They also found one of the bouncers, who was now an old man.

He confirmed there were only two of us. He stated that without any doubt a large group of them had pursued us out of the club with obvious intentions. When asked why he hadn't mentioned this when quizzed at the time, he said he hadn't wanted to get involved as he had only just got out of prison himself. Life, eh? Full of surprises. In the end, he wanted to confess too.

Neither him, nor the boy, could identify a picture of Frank, or the lad who Frank said was with him, so the case collapsed. There was no interest in spending the money on a trial to see if an outnumbered dead man had killed some people who were attacking him three decades ago.

Frank met me on the day I was released, as did my probation worker. I had to spend the following two months in approved premises. It was like a cheap hotel where the only residents were people on ViSOR. This is a database of records of those required to register with the police under the Sexual Offences Act 2003 or those jailed for more than twelve months for violent offences.

They are quiet places, full of worries. There were no games of charades on a Sunday evening.

It was harder than being in prison. To start with, I had to sign in seven times a day, to let them know where I was. There was nothing to do and everyone simmered with tension. Many fell by the wayside and were recalled back to prison. Frank visited daily and kept me going. He's been a brilliant brother, all things considered. Few would have forgiven as he has.

He's here today to pick me up. I'm moving to the seaside; you can imagine my destination. I'll always have hope. Although, I have to register my whereabouts to the authorities and will need to do so until I die. I keep the letter from Kirsty with me at all times. I read it to Frank. He said he believed me anyway but would have stuck by me regardless.

The staff came to wave me off. I showed the manager my letter. She cried, and said, 'But you were in prison for nine years.' Maybe I deserved those nine years. Few of us are guilty of nothing. Perhaps it took nearly a decade behind bars for me to find out who I was.

As for what I was convicted of – you've read my story, so you decide. Was what I did beyond the boundaries of acceptable behaviour? Am I a sick pervert, or just a kind lonely man trying to offer a desperately sad and lost little girl some kindness? In my heart, I know I only had good intentions.

As we drive through the outskirts, I wind the window down. Now, I am free. Next time you are in a bar ordering a pint, take care to look at the man beside you. Do you know what they're thinking? Are they happy? We all fight our own unique battles.

Will I return here? I think that I shall. Strangely, I want to help Kirsty, if she's still around. So, as you sup your beer, I could be the person next to you. Please, say hello.

LIFE

Thank you for reading *Survivor*. An experience at times that was no doubt uncomfortable, as it was writing Vincent's story. I hope there are many thought-provoking points inside, ones that will stay with you as you view and interact with the world.

The concept of liking Vincent is a strange one. It's human nature to look for the positives in the people we read about or meet. We search for similarities and understanding. Some amongst us, but by no means all, have an unlimited capacity for forgiveness. Even for something as terrible as the crimes in this book.

I used to read some of the mail to the prisoners when I worked inside. I watched them at their visits, too. If it was your child or husband who had lost their way, would you cast them out? Could you ignore a letter from one of your parents who wanted to try and explain? Or perhaps it was your best friend whose sins altered your view of the world and made you question your judgement.

I remember a note from a grandmother to her grandson who had knifed his girlfriend to death. It began, 'I know nobody else will have anything to do with you now, and I can't begin to understand what you've done, but you are still my grandson.'

Many people's lives are damaged by unlawful acts, not just those who suffer directly.

Do you believe Vincent was a worthless criminal? He was certainly a victim too.

Like most mental health issues, Borderline Personality Disorder (BPD) is hard to diagnose. Research suggests that genetic, brain, environmental and social factors are causes. BPD is approximately five times more likely to occur if a person has a close family member with the disorder. Many people with the condition have had a traumatic past, such as abuse or abandonment during childhood.

Some have been exposed to unstable relationships and upsetting experiences that have severely affected them. Vincent didn't have an easy life.

The one point I'd like to comment on is the loss of memories. Vincent can't remember anything before the accident. This links with Jake in *Lifer*, who was in a variety of children's homes and foster care.

When we are very young, we don't know who we are. We recognise ourselves from the people who look after us. The people who say, 'You like ice creams,' and, 'You love bunny.' This is usually our parents but it can be anyone who is constantly by our sides.

Remembering is a learned skill. One we haven't mastered when we are little children. Therefore, our carers hold our memories for us. A sense of who we are promotes emotional well-being. Recalling, for example, that being pleasant to other kids means they will be nice back. That is pivotal in our young lives.

Discussing your child's day is an important part of their development. How many times have you asked your youngster what they did today on the way home from school, only for them to say they couldn't remember? We teach them to be storytellers.

Prompting and cajoling the information out of them helps them to form bonds, not just to people, but also to time and places. Explaining, 'We're going to Nanny's today, do you remember last time?' provokes thoughts of who they are and what's important to them. They may shout, 'We had chippies,' or, 'I didn't like the dog.' They are settled as they begin to understand how they fit into life.

If our children aren't nurtured in the correct way, is it any wonder they go off the rails? Once behaviour patterns are set, it's incredibly hard to rewire someone. We must get it right from the start. It isn't about not making mistakes, but more about consistency, routine and patience.

We fear the unknown. Experience is arguably the most valuable commodity in the world. It's what businesses pay big money for. If we know how to react and respond to an event because we have seen it many times before, then we are comfortable and relaxed. We can behave in the right way.

What happens if you can't remember growing up, as in Vincent's case, and nobody reminds you? Imagine how unsettling it would be to have an incomplete past? How about the sad tale of a child going from foster care to a children's home and back again? Who holds those precious memories then?

It's not just the toys that are left behind.

Memories ground us, so our futures may fly.

— ROSS GREENWOOD 2017

ACKNOWLEDGMENTS

I would like to thank, in no particular order, Yvette Smart, Nicola Holmes, Kev Duke, Alex Knell, Rachel Brightey, Mark Blackburn, Kate Symonds, Louise Holmes, Emma De Oliveira, Jo Curtis, Jamie Jones, Steve Mansbridge, Barry Butler, Jono Hill, Kaisha Holloway, Caroline Vincent, Ros Rendle, Jim Ody, Richard Burke and, of course, Amanda Rayner. You all played a part! Alex Williams, yours was a big one.

Please leave a review, it really helps.

MORE FROM ROSS GREENWOOD

We hope you enjoyed reading *Survivor*. If you did, please leave a review.

If you'd like to gift a copy, this book is also available as an ebook, digital audio download and audiobook CD.

Sign up to Ross Greenwood's mailing list for news, competitions and updates on future books.

http://bit.ly/RossGreenwoodNewsletter

Why not explore the DI Barton series.

ABOUT THE AUTHOR

Ross Greenwood is the bestselling author of over ten crime thrillers. Before becoming a full-time writer he was most recently a prison officer and so worked everyday with murderers, rapists and thieves for four years. He lives in Peterborough.

Follow Ross on social media:

twitter.com/greenwoodross
facebook.com/RossGreenwoodAuthor
bookbub.com/authors/ross-greenwood
instagram.com/rossg555

ABOUT BOLDWOOD BOOKS

Boldwood Books is a fiction publishing company seeking out the best stories from around the world.

Find out more at www.boldwoodbooks.com

Sign up to the Book and Tonic newsletter for news, offers and competitions from Boldwood Books!

http://www.bit.ly/bookandtonic

We'd love to hear from you, follow us on social media:

facebook.com/BookandTonic
twitter.com/BoldwoodBooks
instagram.com/BookandTonic

Printed in Great Britain
by Amazon